"No phones. ⬚⬚⬚⬚⬚⬚⬚⬚⬚ no good. We're ⬚⬚⬚⬚⬚⬚⬚ Gab⬚⬚⬚

A sudden, uncon⬚⬚⬚⬚⬚⬚⬚⬚⬚⬚ swept through her. One felt just as she had watching the river sweep away an entire bridge. There was a power at work here that threatened to sweep away any barriers she and Gabe might erect between them, and there'd be no way to avoid being caught again in the maelstrom. He wanted her there. He'd brought her there, knowing they'd be alone, knowing there was no way for her to escape. He still wanted her as much as she wanted him!

"Gabe," she said, "there's got to be some way out of here, a raft, canoe—"

"No. It's pitch black, the river's running like crazy. I won't let you go, Kathy, it's too dangerous."

It was just as dangerous for her to stay!

Gabe reached over and took her hand. She was so cold, and he wanted to warm her, knew he could. "Kathy, don't be afraid to stay here with me."

She felt his warmth, his strength, and was torn between wanting to curl her fingers around his, and to jerk away and run for it. Oh, she was afraid, all right, but not of him. It was a delicious, thrilling fear that she wanted to go curling through her, exciting her, making her blood run hotter and . . .

"If you don't quit looking at me like that, you might have something to be afraid of, after all," he warned her softly.

"Gabe," she whispered. "I've never been afraid of you. Not before, not now, not ever. . . ."

WHAT ARE *LOVESWEPT* ROMANCES?

They are stories of true romance and touching emotion. We believe those two very important ingredients are constants in our highly sensual and very believable stories in the *LOVESWEPT* line. Our goal is to give you, the reader, stories of consistently high quality that may sometimes make you laugh, sometimes make you cry, but are always fresh and creative and contain many delightful surprises within their pages.

Most romance fans read an enormous number of books. Those they truly love, they keep. Others may be traded with friends and soon forgotten. We hope that each *LOVESWEPT* romance will be a treasure—a "keeper." We will always try to publish

LOVE STORIES YOU'LL NEVER FORGET
BY AUTHORS YOU'LL ALWAYS REMEMBER

The Editors

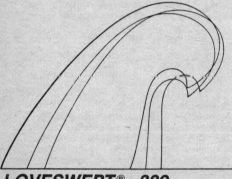

LOVESWEPT® • 389

Judy Gill
Stargazer

BANTAM BOOKS
NEW YORK • TORONTO • LONDON • SYDNEY • AUCKLAND

STARGAZER

A Bantam Book / March 1990

LOVESWEPT® *and the wave device are registered
trademarks of Bantam Books, a division of
Bantam Doubleday Dell Publishing Group, Inc.
Registered in U.S. Patent
and Trademark Office and elsewhere.*

*If you would be interested in receiving protective vinyl
covers for your Loveswept books, please write to this address
for information:*

Loveswept
Bantam Books
P.O. Box 985
Hicksville, NY 11802

ISBN 0-553-44001-2

Published simultaneously in the United States and Canada

PRINTED IN THE UNITED STATES OF AMERICA

OPM   0 9 8 7 6 5 4 3 2 1

For my cousin, K.I.G.
Because it's your turn.

One

Perched on top of her car, Kathy M'Gonigle was
beginning to feel like Snoopy on his doghouse roof.
All she needed to do was exchange her camera bag
for a typewriter: *It was a dark and stormy night . . .*

It *was* a dark and stormy night—well, evening—
and it was getting darker and stormier by the minute. Rain pelted down, making the roof treacherously
slick. Each movement Kathy made threatened to
send her sliding into the deepening flood that now
swirled over the hood of the car, streaming past the
windshield. She'd have to make do with the camera
case, because her lap-top computer was under a foot
of water in the trunk of the car. She thought briefly
about taking out one of the cameras again and trying
to record what appeared to be the last few minutes
of the world's existence, but shook her head at her
own idiocy. End of the world or not, letting go to
take more pictures would certainly mean her end.
No doubt she'd already sacrificed her life getting the
ones she had. She'd known perfectly well it was
crazy to stop, so this predicament was her own fault.
She should have kept going, seeking higher ground.

The danger had been evident to her at least an hour earlier.

Any fool would have seen that the river was rising rapidly, spreading its banks wider and wider—and she was no fool. She'd gotten herself safely across the river and onto the banks of a creek that should have held the overflow quite nicely. However, she'd had no idea that the whole western watershed of the Monashee Mountains had been about to end up in the creek. It was too late then to do anything but try to wait it out, and since she had to wait, why not keep on clicking? She couldn't pass up such an opportunity. After all, it was her livelihood, her life. If she survived, she'd have an incredible record of events during a flood.

It was great stuff, and she was excited. No one else would have photographs like hers or a story to tell of the way the ground had trembled from the force of the water as it tumbled trees and boulders along. Well, maybe one person would.

Just possibly, her father, Mike M'Gonigle, was in some other precarious spot, filling his notebooks or clicking away like mad, recording the storm and the flood for the old-fashioned weekly newspaper he'd been running since before she was born.

Lightning flashed at the same time a huge thunderclap rattled the air around her. Darn, she thought, maybe trying to stay on top of the car was just as dangerous as being spilled off into that disgusting looking brown soup that the river had become in the past hour as it flooded the pleasant little valley she had once called home.

The decision was all but taken from her as the car lurched, and she nearly fell off. Terrified, she found herself spread-eagle, clinging to the small fingerholds at the tops of the windows, her eyes only a short distance from the swirl of water that was now half-way up the windshield. No, she did not want to get into that water. She remembered the deer and bob-cats she'd seen scrambling past her before she realized her escape had been cut off, and wondered if all of those other large objects floating past her were logs and stumps. What if some of them—even one of them—was a bear? She'd rather be on the roof than in the water, she decided.

The car bobbed again and shifted from side to side. She fixed her gaze on a tree. It was getting closer. The car was afloat. Oh, Lordy, how long would that last? Should she hope that she was carried to the tree, so she could get off the car? What if the tree was uprooted or submerged? And there was the lightning. It flashed again. Nope, she didn't want to get into a tree. If people were warned to stay out from under trees during thunderstorms, surely it wasn't safe to get into one of them!

A long, sustained blast of thunder sounded, and she squeezed her eyes shut, clinging to the car, still seeing the simultaneous flashes of lightning that speared the air around her. Coward, she told herself, forcing her eyes open. If it was going to happen, it was going to happen. She'd meet the end with courage and grace.

Unsteadily, she returned to sitting cross-legged on the roof of the car, camera bag between her thighs, fingers gripping the edge of the roof.

A blast of wind nearly flung her from the roof, and the thunder roared even louder. Carefully, she lifted her head and looked up into the rain as she realized that it wasn't thunder she was hearing, nor was she seeing one long flare of lightning. There was a heli-copter above her, and the bright light cutting into the gloom of the storm was from a searchlight at-tached to the chopper's belly. Down that beam, looking like an angel wearing a crash helmet, slid a man on a safety harness who came to a stop with his knees near her chin. Slowly, he came lower until he could reach out and touch her.

For a moment she thought she was hallucinating. It was an angel! Her own personal angel. "Gabriel?" she asked, her voice lost in the roar of the machine above. "Gabe Fowler?" Relief and disbelief and myriad other emotions swirled through her, rendering her momentarily inarticulate.

Not so Gabriel. He obviously was shocked to find her there. It was evident in his voice, in his face, in his words. "What in the hell are you doing here? Of all the stupid, damn-fool places for you to turn up, this beats them all!"

Even as he berated her, he swiftly wrapped a heavy strap around her middle and between her legs, linking her to the cable that attached him to the aircraft above. His mouth taut, his eyes as stormy as the air around them, he avoided her gaze while he worked, and she could only cling to his shoulders, staring at him.

Gabe was home? It seemed impossible, but it really was him, not some dream figure she'd conjured up out of need and fear. Yet, why should she be so surprised? *She* was home, wasn't she? And though her trips back to the valley were rare, it was strange that she'd never run into him, that their visits hadn't coincided before. Their only meeting since they'd both left the valley had taken place four years earlier, but it had been thousands of miles away on the other side of the ocean.

He shoved her camera bag around so that it hung behind her, and gestured to the pilot with one sweeping arm. He began to lift away from her, and, momentarily forgetting the cable to which they were both linked, she clutched at him and felt herself begin to lift too. He held her to him, her chin just above the level of his belt buckle, his hands pinning her close and his thighs wrapped around her in a strangely intimate embrace that should have made her uncomfortable but had the opposite effect. With her cheek pressed to the hardness of his belly, she tipped her head back and looked up at him. His face, with the white helmet surrounding it, was in shadow, but she sensed that he was staring at her, and she managed a smile. If he smiled back, she couldn't tell, but he pressed a hand to the side of her head, offering silent reassurance as they slowly were drawn up into the opening in the body of the helicopter. There, another man grabbed them and helped them regain their footing before slamming the door and taking a seat in the front of the aircraft beside the pilot.

Gabe unhooked himself and then Kathy from the cable before pressing her into a seat. As the helicopter turned, banking sharply, he flopped into a seat beside her, reaching out to snap a seat belt around her, his head buzzing with the shock of finding Kathy in the middle of the flood, with the horror of knowing how close she had been to dying, with the incomparable joy of being able to touch her again, see her, hear her voice. Sensing her eyes on him, he met her gaze, saw that she was as stunned as he at this turn of events—and as much at a loss for words. It was just as well, because he didn't think he'd be capable of saying anything civil to her, even if the noise level in the chopper had permitted polite conversation. Apart from everything else he felt about her, rage over her utter stupidity topped the list.

Tearing his gaze from hers, he plugged his helmet into the intercom with trembling hands and spoke quickly to the pilot, then gripped the armrests so tightly his knuckles ached. It was either do that or strangle her.

Kathy lifted one shaking hand and wiped ineffectually at the water running from her hair into her eyes, as she tried to get a better look at Gabe. He had such a hold on the arms of his seat that she expected to see the metal bend. His eyes, pale brown with golden lights, glittered angrily into hers while a muscle leapt in his temple and the dimple high up under one eye contracted into a tense little pucker. He shouted something she couldn't hear, but she thought she picked up the words "home" and "soon," so she settled back into her seat. Home soon was good enough for her. Gabe's fury she would deal with when it became necessary.

Home. Kathy felt a flutter of excitement well up inside her as the helicopter lurched and slid sideways through the air on a downward angle. As it righted itself, the noise increased to a horrendous crescendo that even the gentle thump of their landing failed to break.

Almost there. Almost home, she thought. And wasn't Mike M'Gonigle going to be one surprised man!

Gabe took off his helmet, unfastened his safety harness, then undid hers. With a tap on the pilot's shoulder, and a quick handshake for the copilot who had left his seat to swing open the door in the side of the craft, he leapt to the ground below and held up his arms to Kathy.

Unhesitatingly, she launched herself out and down, confident Gabriel would catch her. He did, and they cleared away quickly from the helicopter so it could take off again, clawing its way into the stormy air. Kathy lifted her head, looked around, and came to a halt.

She was the one who was surprised.

"Why have you brought me here?" she asked, slinging her case back around to the front. They were only a couple of hundred yards from Gabe's family's hilltop home.

Taking her arm and walking fast, he steered her toward the house, their feet squishing in the soggy grass. In truth, he hadn't thought. He'd merely reacted. Kathy was back in the valley. He lived in this house. It was where he had to bring her. "Because every evacuation center is crammed to the rafters," he improvised, still marching her along. "The whole damn valley's under water, or haven't you noticed?"

"But my dad—"

"Will be just fine. He's likely to be camped out in one of the schools as any intelligent person would be." His grip on her arm was tight, almost painful, and she was close to tripping as she ran to keep up with his long strides. Gabriel Fowler was in a temper, that was for sure, and she wasn't certain she wanted to hang around while he worked out whatever was bothering him. He'd been in a dark and brooding mood the last time she'd seen him, when he'd walked out of her shipboard cabin just as dawn had streaked through the porthole. It seemed his disposition hadn't improved any in four years.

He nearly lifted her up the steps onto the back porch and out of the driving rain.

"If you don't mind, I'd rather be with Dad," she said, wrenching free as Gabe swung the door open. "I'll be just fine wherever he is."

"I don't know where he is. I'm only guessing." Gabe shoved her through the door in front of him and slammed it against the wind and rain. He reached over her shoulder to turn on a light, and she blinked in the sudden brightness. Looping the broad strap of her camera bag over her head, she set the heavy carrier onto the table in the center of the room.

"Now suppose you tell me exactly what in the hell you were doing out there?" said Gabe, his big hands locking onto her shoulders, squeezing water from the sodden down in her jacket.

"Hello, Gabriel," she said, her eyes flaring. "It's nice to see you too."

"Do't play games with me! To my knowledge, the Mounties had every back road blocked off hours before there was any danger! What did you do, take the law into your own hands and sneak around the end of a roadblock?"

Bringing her fists up quickly, she knocked his hands aside. "I sneaked around nothing!" she snapped. "I didn't see any roadblocks, and if I had, I'd have had sense enough not to pass them!"

"You were crazy not to seek higher ground sooner!"

As mad at herself as she was at him, she shoved away from him and would have strode past him, but he caught her elbow and swung her around so their bodies were touching. His chest was rising and falling rapidly. Her breasts lifted against him with the force of her own breathing. Something electric leapt between them for a moment, and she wanted to laugh and cry and swear at him all at the same time, but instead she snatched her arm free and walked away.

"Don't touch me," she said in a low, quivering growl filled with the passion and excitement she couldn't help feeling, emotions she knew by the glitter in his eyes that he shared.

He ignored her order, or accepted it as a challenge, clamping his hands on her shoulders again, outlining her collarbone through the layers of fabric with his thumbs. "You seemed glad enough to have my hands on you when I rescued you from that flood."

"I'd have been glad to see anybody at that time!"

"And you damn well should have been!" he told her. "It was a miracle we found you, you know. On an impulse we decided to check the bridge over Massey Creek on our way home. Then we saw that the river had backed up into the creek and the damn bridge was gone. We were about to fly on when Jim shouted."

He closed his eyes tightly for a second and drew in a harsh breath. "I'll never know how he spotted the tiny bit of brightness your red jacket created on the roof of the brown car in the brown water. Dammit, Kathy, what kind of stupid reason could you have for being there just at that time?"

"I was working, if you must know. And everything happened too fast for me to do much about it."

"*Working?*"

She stood with her balled up fists on her hips, and tilted her chin up. "Yes, Gabriel. Working. I do that for a living, you know."

When he spoke again, fear and anger still tautened his voice. "Your work! Is that still all you care about? Aren't you aware of the danger you were in? I turn cold just thinking how close you came to dying today!"

"Yes, I'm aware of the danger I was in, and I do know how close I came to dying. But I didn't die! Instead I got some incredible shots of that river in action," she said, feeling again the excitement and the power and the fear she had experienced in the flood. Looking at him, she wondered if there were any way to convey to him just what she had felt. It seemed important somehow that she make him understand how it had been. Quickly, she opened her camera bag, took out the two cameras, the tape recorder and casettes, the floppy disks from her computer, and several canisters of film, littering the table with her gear.

"What I have on these films," she said, waving a hand over the black canisters, "is the real, as-it-happens situation—trees and branches and boulders sweeping by the side of the road! And I got some fantastic pictures of animals in flight from the danger; deer and raccoons and cats of some kind, even a little brown rabbit and a couple of porcupines, all swimming and clawing for safety, oblivious of my presence, scrambling up right beside me, leaping into the bush. Lord, I'll never forget the panic in their eyes! Wild animals that would normally have seen me as a danger, ignoring me in the face of a greater peril! I caught the bridge—the one near where you found me—at its very moment of disintegration, as it collapsed under the weight of debris and rush of water. And the noise, Gabriel! The noise of boulders tumbling and grinding and shaking the earth! You should have seen it, heard it, felt it!"

Eyes shining, fatigue and fear forgotten, she patted her tape recorder. "I've got it all, along with my thoughts and feelings. If only there had been some way to can the vibrations I felt under the car when the bridge started to go."

"Good Lord!" The way he said it, it was a prayer for strength. He leaned forward, his fists on the table as if he would crush her recorder, her cameras—maybe her. "You were on that bridge when it collapsed?"

"No. No, I felt it start to shake as I drove over it, and as soon as I was clear, I stopped to watch and photograph it. What a scene! Mother Nature outdoing Dante."

He stared at her angrily, his eyes narrowed. "You

make it sound like a professional coup, for heaven's sake!"

"But it was!" she said just as hotly. "I can get a great article out of this, Gabe. Several articles, probably. Maybe it'll get me a cover on *National Geographic* or *Equinox*."

"Is that what you were thinking about when the water came up around your car? A cover on *Equinox*?"

She shrugged and tried to ignore the accusation she heard in his voice. "No. Not exactly. Not specifically. But I was immersed in my work. Uh—no pun intended," she said with a sheepish smile to which Gabe did not respond as he once would have. "Well, dammit, I don't care if you do disapprove. I love my work, and I'm proud of what I was able to do. That's what's important to me."

"Yes," he said, and nodded curtly, his jaw still knotted so tightly it pulsed. "I know that."

"Why do you care?" she challenged. "Work's what's important to you too. Or is it okay for you but not for me? Is it safe being dangled out of a helicopter on a skinny little cable?"

"You'd better get down on your knees tonight and thank God that I was there to dangle on that skinny little cable, Kathy M'Gonigle! And while you're at it, thank him for the sharp eyes of the copilot, because without him, you'd be halfway to the Pacific Ocean now, as dead as you are stupid!"

Kathy flew at him, but he caught her upper arms, holding her off.

On one level she was aware that he was enjoying this battle as much as she was, that in some way it was necessary to both of them, but she was too angry to think it through.

"Don't you call me stupid, Gabriel Fowler!" she flared. "If I'd known there was any real danger, I'd have gotten myself out in time. It all happened too fast," she said again. "But I was not trapped through any stupidity on my part."

He was grinning now. "Okay, okay, I'm sorry. I should have remembered how much you hate that word. You're not stupid. Reckless, maybe. Foolhardy. Rash and overly eager to point your damned cameras and babble into your tape recorder, but not stupid."

Her show of temper may have dwindled, but her eyes remained hot and two splotches of color stained her cheeks. "Thank you for that much, at least."

His grin faded, and he blew out a long, shuddering sigh. Kathy saw the last remains of his anger go out with it, as his hand curled warmly over the back of her neck. "Oh, Kathy," he whispered raggedly. "Of all the ways to find you again . . ."

He touched her soft, short hair, feeling the silk of its dark wet strands under his fingers. It was almost masculinely short, but on her it looked good, somehow adding to her femininity.

"Find me again? Why, Gabriel, I'm flattered. I had no idea you were even looking for me."

"Kath, I hate to hear you being sarcastic and cold."

"You get what you give," she said.

"Hey, cool down. I said I was sorry, and I meant my apology." He cupped her chin, feeling the faint quivering of her flesh. "I'd forgotten just how quick being called stupid could make you mad. But you don't seem to realize just how close you came to dying, and thinking about it scares me all over again."

She leaned into his palm for an instant before sitting down on one of the oak chairs in response to the sudden weakening of her knees. His hand fell to his side. "And Gabriel scared is Gabriel mad," she said. "All right. I remember that little axiom. Apology accepted."

"Thanks. Now, get out of those wet things. You must be freezing."

"Get out of them and into what?" she asked, pulling a little plastic package from a side pocket of her bag. It contained the change of underwear she always carried there. "This seems to comprise my entire wardrobe." She grinned and pulled out another couple of little bags. "And my toiletries." A comb, toothbrush, toothpaste, and a small tube of lipstick followed.

Again, Gabe looked less than pleased. "You told me four years ago, that night aboard the *Orion*, that you traveled light," he said tautly, taking a chair at her side. "I didn't realize how literally you meant it."

He didn't seem to find it necessary to stipulate which night, she noticed, and she wasn't surprised. Because while for him there must have been endless starry nights, both before and after those they'd shared, she knew that night had been special for both of them. If it had ended differently, their lives might have been changed forever. She suppressed a sigh. Gabe hadn't wanted his life changed forever. He had the life he'd sought—the life of a sailor, first in the Navy, then as an officer of the cruise line. And she . . . she'd been nothing more than the girl he'd had to leave behind in order to find that life.

"You said then that material things weren't important to you," he reminded her, breaking into her thoughts. "I guess that hasn't changed."

She remembered saying that, remembered trying to hide from him the need she had to burrow deeper into his arms and beg him to let her spend the rest of her life with him. But, because of the life he had chosen, she'd known that, emotionally, he must travel light, so she'd used the phrase to describe her own life, hiding behind it. Even now she did the same.

"Things aren't important, Gabe. They can be re-

placed. At least some things can. The products of
my mind, what I write, what I photograph would be
harder to replace, so they were what I most wanted
to save."

"What about people? Are they important to you?"

"Yes, of course." She frowned, perplexed. Gabe
knew that. "I came home because I'm worried about
my dad. I think he might be sick, or maybe having
business problems."

Gabe started at her words. Sick? Business problems? For the love of heaven, didn't Kathy *know*?
He looked into her clear green eyes, seeing the worry
and concern for her father, but that was all. For a
moment he let himself search for the emotions he'd
grown used to seeing in the eyes of women who
knew who he was, what had happened, but Kathy
looked at him as she always had—openly, trustingly.
No flicker of fear. No pity. No . . . speculation.

"Gabe? What is it? You're looking at me strangely."
Alarm flared in her eyes. "My dad? There is something wrong? Something you know about?"

"No, no. Nothing's wrong with him," he denied,
but something in his face told her he was lying.

"Tell me," she said, leaning toward him, her eyes
beseeching. "Please, I have to know."

"I . . . I don't know," he lied, but she wasn't about
to let him get away with that.

"You do! You can't hide it from me." She lifted one
cold hand and touched his cheek. "Oh, please," she
said again. "We've been friends too long for you to lie
to me."

Friends? He caught her hand and moved it, holding it on the table between them, conscious of its
fragility. Yet what else could they be to one another?
Although they had loved each other years before
when Kathy had been too young and he had been
too restless to settle down, friendship was all that

was possible for him to offer her now in spite of that one magical, beautiful, perfect night when they had been lovers.

Now, he had to accept that they had that uncomfortable, edgy, difficult relationship of former lovers—and he didn't want it to be that way at all. His heart hammered hard in his chest. His breathing grew labored. With effort, he controlled that. His heart he couldn't slow, not with Kathy in the same room, because no matter what, he still had such a craving for her, he thought he might go mad. He dropped her hand, shoved his chair back, and moved quickly away from her, putting half the room between them before turning back and risking another glance at her.

"Gabe? What's wrong?" Kathy followed him, not about to be put off. "It *is* Daddy, isn't it? Is he—" Panic flared in her eyes, her face paled, and she swayed.

"No!" he said quickly, holding her shoulders in his hands, giving her an impatient little shake when really it was himself he was impatient with. "Kathy, believe me, Mike is fine. I promise you. He's as healthy as you are."

Though, he wondered, exactly how healthy was that? She was terribly thin. "As healthy as I am," he amended, gentling his hold on her. She may have been thin, but she was still too damned appealing to him. Always had been. Always would be. Below the sodden red jacket she wore, the jacket that had very likely saved her life, her wet jeans clung to slim hips and very feminine, tapering thighs. Her high-top pink sneakers were a childish touch that made him want to laugh and, in the next breath, made him want to hug her. Instead, he set his face and mind into stern control, suddenly afraid that if he hugged her, kissed her, she'd disappear like a puff of smoke.

It would be Singapore and the *Orion* all over again. She was still so beautiful and so special to him that he wanted to grab her and run from this place, from all the people and events that could and would interfere with them, from the fears that had kept him silent years ago when he had ached so badly to tell her how he felt, to ask her to share his life.

Her frown drew a deep line between her brows, and for the first time he thought she looked close to her age of thirty-one. "And how healthy is that?" she asked. "You don't look so great, you know."

He drew in a deep breath and let her stand unsupported. "I'm just tired and maybe still a little shocked that it was you I found on the roof of that car. Last I heard you were in South America somewhere."

"I got back from there more than a month ago. And if you think you're surprised and shocked, how do you think I feel?" she asked. "Last time I saw you, you were striding around the deck of a cruise liner in the Orient, looking gorgeous and official and very nautical in that white uniform with all the gold braid. And where is your beard?"

She lifted her hand toward his clean-shaven chin. To avoid her touch, he moved quickly away from her to shuck his worn cowboy boots. The boots teetered for a moment, then fell over, one going east, the other going west, but he ignored them as he unzipped his orange coveralls. She watched him move, mesmerized.

Even with the loss of those inches afforded by the heels of his boots, dropped down to his barefoot five eleven, he was an impressive man. She licked suddenly dry lips and drew in a shaky breath.

"Get out of those wet things," he said again, glancing over at her, but Kathy continued to watch him, all at once too weak and exhausted to comply—and too fascinated, too caught up in memories.

Underneath the coveralls, his shirt and jeans were soaked, too, clinging to him in a manner she found quite intriguing. He unbuttoned the shirt, and off it came, revealing shoulders that were no surprise to her at all, not in their breadth, their muscular hardness, nor their rich brown color. His chest was powerful with only a tiny sprinkling of hair down its center, and his belly, above the low-cut jeans, was flat and hard, ridged with muscles. Muscles she remembered very well, as her warm cheeks attested.

He was completely unself-conscious as he stood there rubbing his russet hair with his shirt, his gaze on her, one eyebrow lifted, his mouth curved into a half-smile.

She still didn't move, so he stepped to where she stood and unzipped her down jacket, seeing with a frown how tiny she was under the clinging, wet fabric of her pale blue blouse.

"You're too skinny," he said.

She only nodded.

"Have you been sick?" His hand lifted of its own volition and touched one wisp of the short black hair that hung in little ringlets on her forehead.

"No. I've just been working hard." Kathy stood very still as he drew a rough thumb across her cheek just below her left eye, then lower, to the corner of her mouth.

"Your eyes look like big, green marbles," he said, his voice suddenly very low. "They never looked so big before." Or so hungry, or so bewildered, or so sad. *Oh, Kathy,* he said silently, *why did you have to come back here and put us both through all this emotional turmoil again?* As if she knew what he was thinking, she looked down and took a step backward.

He saw the shivers that shook her, and ached with the need to tilt her face up to his again, to continue looking into her beautiful eyes, to hold her, and warm her and love her, but he resisted the temptation with every bit of strength he had. "Hurry up," he said gruffly, turning from her. "Take that jacket off. I'll run you a tub." Again toweling his hair with his shirt, he hurried away from her while he still could.

Two

Awkwardly, finding her fingers now swollen and all but useless, their tips bruised from having clung to the gutters at the sides of the car, Kathy peeled the jacket off and dumped it into one of the sinks, seeing through the window that dark had fallen outside. Silver streaks obscured even the most minimal view, and the light from the room reflected back into her eyes. Wearily, she followed the sound of running water and entered the bathroom where the tub was already half-full with frothing bubbles. Gabe was not in sight.

With a sigh, Kathy closed the door, stripped, and slid into the surrounding heat of the water, stretching out so her toes touched the end of the tub to keep her from sinking completely. She closed her eyes and quickly drifted off.

"Hey, don't go to sleep, for pete's sake!" Gabe's voice brought her eyes only half-open, but the sight of him wearing faded jeans and a thick gray sweatshirt that did nothing to disguise his impressive chest and shoulders, snapped them wide. Bending, he shut off the water that was about to create another flood—this one across the bathroom floor. Then, sitting on the edge of the tub, he smiled at her.

He smiled and something flipped over inside her, compelling her to reach up and touch him. Needing an excuse, she placed one finger on the dimple under his eye. No, not a dimple, she reminded herself. A scar. From where his half-brother, Art, had poked him with a sharp stick. "How are you getting along with your brother? Or haven't you been here long enough to start rasping against him yet?" She suppressed a shudder, remembering how cruel Art had been and how Gabriel had hated the man. He hadn't, she knew, been alone in that. Very few people could find any good in Art Fowler.

Inwardly, Gabe cursed Mike M'Gonigle for not having told Kathy even the basics of the disaster that had struck the Fowlers. He caught her hand and held it against his face for just a couple of heartbeats but let it go when she pulled gently. He slid along the edge of the tub until he sat near where her pink polished toenails poked out of the bubbles. Suddenly a totally inappropriate surge of relief washed over him because she didn't know about Art. It was a stupid reaction, he told himself in the next second, because it wasn't something he could keep her from finding out, nor was there any reason why he should. Except, of course, because he always had and always would feel guilty, because it had really started years before, when he had been a kid. If he had spoken up the first time he'd suspected Art had struck, his brother wouldn't have had a chance to do it again.

He felt a weight of anger and grief and horror inside him, and the question he'd asked so many times, If I had told someone then, would this have happened? played over and over in his head.

"My brother's not here," he said finally, and to

Kathy his voice sounded taut, strange, and his eyes held her gaze with an intensity she found impossible to read.

"Oh." There was something there she couldn't quite get a handle on, something creating tension in Gabriel, and it tightened her own nerves to the breaking point. It wasn't the sexual tension that had enhanced their anger of before, but it was equally as disturbing. "Where is he?" To her knowledge, Art had never taken a vacation in his life.

"He's . . ." Gabe swallowed. Why was this so hard? Everyone knew about it. There was no reason for Kathy not to know. Yet, he felt such deep shame that he couldn't go on with the story. Clearly, Mike hadn't told her a word of it, and she'd seen no local papers when it all had happened. But why hadn't her father said anything? Oh, hell, he could guess at the reason for Mike's silence, couldn't he? Maybe Mike felt, though he shouldn't, as much shame and pain as Gabe did—and his mother and his sister, Rachel. How could one man's actions have hurt so many innocent people, to say nothing of Art's poor victims and their families? Oh, yes, he had a lot to answer for, Art did. And Gabe.

"Art . . . doesn't live here anymore," he said.

"What?" Kathy nearly sat up, but remembered she was in a tubful of water and bubbles and as naked as a jaybird. "Then who's running the farm?"

"I am. I live here now, Kathy. I'm running the farm for my mother. I've been back a few years now."

Her breath left her in a rush that sent a little puff of bubbles flying through the air to land on the knee of Gabe's jeans. The bubbles sat there, slowly popping until they had disappeared, leaving a tiny damp mark. "Live here?" she asked, her thoughts as solid as the bubbles had been, coming, going, winking in and out of existence as confusion filled her mind.

"But . . . *why*? Oh, Gabe, why? When you always hated it so!"

"I got married. I have a son."

Kathy's mouth went dry and her blood roared in her ears, sounding the way a tidal wave must sound to a clam. Did clams have ears? she thought with a wild attempt to regain sanity. He had just told her he was married, yet he was sitting there on the edge of the tub looking at her as if she were the banana under the cream in the split dish!

It was the last night of the Far East cruise all over again, but there was no dock coming up in Singapore, no means of escape from the terrible pain. There was nothing and no one but her and Gabe and her crazily beating heart and that hungry, needful look in his eyes. She couldn't even begin to offer him understanding because she didn't understand anything of what he was telling her.

She felt hurt, betrayed, sick to her stomach, and she wanted to scream at him. How could he have told her so casually, so callously, that he had married someone else, when all these years she had been waiting for him, believing—no, *knowing*—that someday, when he was ready, he would return to her, make a life with her? Hadn't he said that if he were ever to marry anyone, it would be her? Oh, he hadn't asked her to wait. Never that. In fact, he'd told her not to, told her to find someone else to lavish all her love on. But he hadn't meant it! She'd known that with every part of her that was capable of knowing anything. Oh, Lord, how could she have been so wrong for so long?

Her every instinct said "Hide!" said "Run!" But there was nowhere to hide, nowhere to run, so all she could do was conceal the agony that was coursing through her soul behind a cool she did not feel.

From somewhere, she found the strength and the

presence of mind to say calmly, "Married? You? What a surprise! And here all along everyone was sure you weren't the marrying kind. Tell me about her, Gabe. Is she someone I know?"

He shook his head, unable to force even one word past the tightness in his throat. She was acting, pretending that it didn't matter, but her face was the color of putty, and her green eyes were dark, full of hurt—the same kind of hurt he knew he'd be feeling if she had just given him the identical news about herself.

Kathy managed a big, cheerful smile. At least she hoped it looked big and cheerful, not small and pinched and painful, the way it felt. "Where are they?" she went on. "And how old is your son?"

Gabe gazed at her, wondering how she could do what she was doing, pretend the way she was pretending. It was alien to everything he'd ever known her to be, but maybe that was what she had learned in the years they'd been apart—to hide her hurts, not give people power over her. He admired her courage even while he despised himself for what he was doing to her. Was it the earlier hurts he'd dealt her that had taught her subterfuge could be used as a defense?

He'd never liked hurting her, but he'd known there could never be anything permanent between him and Kathy, that there shouldn't have been anything even temporary. And he'd had to tell that to a sixteen-year-old girl whose kisses were sweeter than honey, even though he'd wanted her then so badly, he'd almost died of it.

"My wife—my ex-wife—isn't here. My son is staying with a friend to free me up for rescue work."

Ex-wife? Kathy's head spun. That Gabe was married was just barely believable. That Gabe was divorced was so far from possible that her mind simply tried to reject it. Gabriel Fowler would never have made a commitment to a woman unless he knew that it was for keeps. Which left one thing: His marriage was over because his ex-wife had made it so. She felt sick again but managed to say, "Your son lives with you?"

"Of course. Where else?"

"Well, with his mother, maybe?" She knew a few divorced people, and mostly it was the mothers who had custody. "Do you have him with you all the time, or do you share custody?"

Gabe's eyes took on a hard look and his jaw knotted. "He lives with me permanently."

"I see." She didn't. And suddenly she didn't want to talk about this anymore. She didn't want to know about his marriage, why it had happened, why it had failed. She wanted to sink under the water and forget about everything. She wanted, she thought, to die inside quietly and without a witness.

As if sensing her need to be alone, Gabe got to his feet and pointed to a bathrobe hanging behind the door. "You can put that on when you get out. Don't be long, okay? I'm warming up some of Mom's good homemade soup." Picking up her wet clothing, he went to the door.

"I won't be long," she said, and wondered if her voice sounded as dead to him as it did to her. The thought of soup, even Grace Fowler's homemade soup, increased her nausea.

Gabe stood looking at her a few moments longer, as if trying to read her expression and her mood, but then turned and went out, closing the door behind him.

Finally alone, she let the pain rise up in her, rocking with its force, her arms wrapped around herself as she cried silently, thoughts and images crowding her brain. She wanted to clear her mind, not think about it at all, but the thoughts kept forming, growing larger and louder in her imagination until they were shouting the facts at her.

Gabe had married, married someone he obviously must have loved deeply. Loved, as he had never loved her. She was forced to acknowledge that in spite of the pain it brought. Why had she never seen before that what Gabe felt for her had nothing to do with the finer emotions? The desire, pure and deep and rich, that had bound them together for those short years in their youth hadn't been love on his part. Love was what she felt. Had felt. Still did? No. Love didn't last all that time. It couldn't. Love needed to be nurtured, cultivated, reciprocated for it to grow. So what she felt for Gabe was not love. Not now.

Then what was it? she asked herself, getting out of the tub and wrapping herself in the big, soft towel, slowly rubbing it over her still-cold skin. Was it just one emotion he caused her to feel? Of course not. Where he was concerned, so very many of her emotions mingled together, she'd never be able to sort them out.

There was desire, of course, as clear and as sharp as ever. And there was a deep longing for something that had once been, a habit she had never tried very hard to break because it was easier just to tell herself that someday it would all work out. And there was anger and hurt and jealousy.

Well, yearning for Gabe was a habit she was going to have to break now that she knew he was capable of loving someone else, of saying those words to someone else, words which, when she had said them to him had made him leave her bed. He'd left her alone and broken and oddly ashamed, feeling, somehow, that she had wronged him by saying them.

Her knees grew weak and she sat down on the side of the tub, her face in her hands, shoulders shaking. What was the matter with her? Why was she so hurt, so angry? She had no real right to be either. This wasn't Gabriel's fault. It never had been. If he had been capable of loving her the way she had loved him, of marrying her, he would have done so. That he had married another woman meant that a future for them wasn't possible.

For several minutes she crouched on the side of the tub, fighting the anguish that snaked through her as she thought of the things that were, the things that had been, the things that would never, ever be. Because, no matter how she tried to pretend, to convince herself otherwise, the fact was that she was still deeply, irretrievably in love with Gabriel Fowler. And loving him as she did, she would settle for nothing less than equal depth of emotion on his part.

When she was able, she splashed her face with cold water, dried it carefully, then slipped into the red velour robe he had offered her. It smelled of Gabe.

"Where is your mother?" she asked minutes later as she sat down and accepted the bowl of steaming vegetable soup Gabe placed before her. "Is she living with Art? And where—?"

He shoved a plate of bread closer to her. "She's down at Rachel's." He sat opposite her and picked up his spoon, taking a bite before lifting his eyes to hers and saying, "We're alone here, you know."

She was startled by his tone. "I realized that. It doesn't worry me. Did you think I needed a warning or something, Gabe? Chaperons are out of date. Aren't you forgetting that I'm thirty-one now? And we spent a lot of unchaperoned time together when I was seventeen—to say nothing of sixteen too." *And twenty-seven.*

"It wasn't a warning," he said, calling himself a

damned liar. He didn't think she needed any warnings, but he sure as hell did. She walked into the room, and his libido went wild. No other woman had ever been able to do that to him, only Kathy. "It was simply a statement of fact." And it had successfully distracted her from asking him anything more about Art. "And I know very well how grown-up you are. I don't suppose you've regressed any in the past four years." He was out of his mind, torturing himself with that memory! And with thoughts of how she had learned the things she had learned, in whose arms, when? And how much more had she learned since?

That was a challenge, and she met it. Of course he was thinking about the time they'd shared aboard the ship *Orion*. On one level, she'd been thinking of little else since he'd scooped her out of the flood, and she suspected that it was the same for him. "I don't suppose I have." Four years before, she had shown him exactly how much growing up she'd done, only it had made no difference to him. He'd still rejected her in the end.

"I saw the series of articles you wrote from your research on the ship," he said.

She glanced at him. "Oh? And were you suitably impressed?"

"They were better than I expected," he admitted grudgingly, she thought, but smiled to hide her hurt. There was, she knew, no pleasing Gabe anymore. Not for her, at any rate.

"That wasn't difficult, I'm sure. You didn't expect any kind of quality work from me at that time."

Her smile cut into him like a sharp knife, and he jerked his gaze away from hers. "It wasn't the quality of your writing I doubted," he said, looking down at the table. "It was the quality of the material you had to work with that concerned me." He flicked a glance back at her face. "You did a good job in spite of that," he said, his praise sounding stiff to his own ears.

"Thanks." She remembered his disapproval when he'd learned that she was to interview and write about the wealthy and famous passengers of the cruise liner on which he was first mate. He'd thought that she was prostituting her talent writing about shallow people with unreal lives. One in particular had bothered him, the Austrian ski star Dieter Krantz.

As if she had said the man's name aloud, Gabe now asked, "Do you still see that German?"

Briefly, Kathy considered pretending she didn't know who he was talking about, but game playing was something she'd never been good at. "Dieter? He was Austrian, and no, I haven't seen him for a couple of years. Have you?"

His eyes widened with a flare of anger as he bit out, "No. Of course not." He got to his feet, lifted the pot of soup, and brought it back to the table. "More?" he asked.

"No, thanks." It was all she could do to keep down the few bites she had taken. Why did she have to ache for him so much, want him so much? It was self-destructive and foolish. She'd be better off back out in the flood, swimming for her life.

While Gabe ladled more of the thick, rich soup into his own bowl, then poured coffee for both of them, Kathy sat back and remembered. She'd eaten many meals at this table as a little girl, when Gabe's sister, Rachel, had been her best friend, and then later when it was Gabe she had come to be with.

"How is Rachel?" she asked, thinking childhood memories might dispel some of the more potent ones that were making her body ache with wanting. "I've missed her."

"Rachel's fine," Gabe said. "I'm sure she misses you too. I suppose you know she lives out on the coast now."

Kathy wasn't so sure that Rachel even remembered her, but all she said was, "Dad told me she had a little boy a couple of years ago."

"That's right. Danny." So, he thought. It seemed Mike had told Kathy some things about the Fowler family. "She's just had another little boy," he continued. "Three weeks ago. That's why Mom's out there with her."

Kathy smiled. "Good for Rachel," she said. "What did they name this one?"

"Matthew. For Dad."

Her smile died. "Oh!" she blurted, "but that was sup—" She broke off. "That's . . . nice," she amended lamely.

"Of course I do. But . . . when we were kids playing house, Rachel always said that you'd claimed first chance at that name for your first son." That had been in the days before Kathy had come to love Gabe, in the days before she had dreamed that her first son would be Matthew, too, after Gabe's long-dead father.

"Yes, well, things change. My son's name is Richard —Ricky. That was his mother's wish." He finished his soup in tense silence, then shoved his bowl aside as he leaned against the back of his chair and looked at her from expressionless eyes.

"What else did your dad tell you about my family?"

"Nothing. Why? What should he have told me?" *Besides the fact that you were married and living in the valley again and still just as able to tear my heart from my body and hold it pumping in your hands.* "He only mentioned Rachel because we used to be such good friends." *And never mentioned you because he knew how much hearing about you hurt me.*

Kathy curled her hands around her coffee cup. "You know," she said wistfully, "I thought we'd always be good friends, but when she got married, she quit writing to me."

"Yes." He shrugged, knowing that this, too, was something that could be laid at his door. "Well, people, like circumstances, change too. Maybe she thought a free-living, roving photojournalist like you wouldn't be interested in the doings of a stay-at-home wife and mother."

"Rachel's I would have been interested in," she said sharply, sensing that Gabe was glad his sister had quit writing to her.

"Maybe before you leave the province again you can get down to the coast to see her," he suggested.

She drew in a deep breath. It was time she told him. "I'm not leaving the province, Gabe. I'm not leaving the valley. I've come home for good. I think my dad needs me here." She set her shoulders back, praying that she was wrong, that when she talked to him, Mike would be able to convince her that she shouldn't stay, that he was as happy and contented as always, releasing her from the need to remain there with him. Because how could she stay now that she knew Gabe was here?

"No!" he said, and she knew that their living near each other would be as difficult for him as it would be for her. "You can't!"

"I'm going to. I . . . want to."

"You'd hate it." It was a statement that came out hard and brusque, but Lord, the thought of sharing the valley with her sent him into a tailspin, a worse one than he'd already been in simply by seeing her again. His heart pounded. Then he realized that of course she wouldn't stay. She'd come there thinking that it was business worries affecting her father, or his health. Once she knew the truth, she'd be on her way again, and probably Mike with her. As if to remind himself more firmly that her continued stay in the valley was not to be, he said, "You won't last more than a month. Not now. Like me, you've seen the world and what it has to offer. You told me last time we were together that the valley was a trap we'd both been lucky to escape. You won't be content here now."

Oh, wouldn't she? she thought. Under the right circumstances, she would. But aloud, she said, "Of course I will. I grew up in this valley. It was my home once; surely I can make it my home again." Her silent *You did* hung between them. "I'll be just as happy here as I ever was. All right, all right," she held up a hand to forestall whatever he might have been about to say. "I'm glad I left when I did. I needed to go away from here, but now I need to come back for Mike's sake. I told you, I sense that something is troubling him." She got to her feet. "Where did you take my clothes? I'd better put them in the dryer so I can get changed. I really do want to get down there tonight." She went to the wall phone above a cluttered desk in the corner. "I'll phone Dad right now, and he can come and get me."

"No."

She whirled and met his gaze. "What do you mean, 'no'?"

"The phones are out, Kathy. I'm afraid you're stuck here."

"Then will you drive me down? Or lend me a car?"

"No," he said. "I told you, we're marooned." His eyes were half-lidded, and he smiled faintly, watching her. She knew his tone of regret was phony.

A sudden, uncontrollable thrill of excitement swept through her. She felt just as she had watching the power of the river sweep away an entire bridge. There was a power at work that threatened to sweep away any barriers she and Gabe might erect between them, and she didn't see any way to avoid being caught up in the maelstrom again. He wanted her there. He had brought her there knowing they'd be alone, knowing there was no way for her to escape. He still wanted her as much as she wanted him. There was no way he could hide it, and he wasn't trying to. He may have married someone else, but he still wanted Kathy M'Gonigle!

Her heart beat high in her throat. "Marooned. I . . . see."

He set his smoldering gaze on her, and she met it. "Do you?" he asked. "Do you understand that I brought you here because I couldn't bear the thought of your being anywhere else?"

She nodded, gripping the edge of the desk with one hand, the phone with the other. "I also understand that feeling that way doesn't make you happy."

"No. No, it doesn't, but I can't find a way to change it. Can you?"

She hardened herself, wishing she had the ability to lie with ease, to tell him that she didn't feel what he knew she felt. "I mean to tr—" She broke off, lifting her chin an inch. "I don't intend to give in to it."

"Good luck."

Then, even though she believed him, she lifted the phone and listened for a dial tone. Nothing. As if he could right things for her, she said pleadingly, "I have to get to Mike tonight. Surely you can understand that." Of course he was as aware of the tremor in her voice as she was, and as aware of the reason. "Do you have a rubber raft, a canoe, anything like that here?"

He just shook his head in disgust. "It's pitch black

outside, and the river's running like crazy. Don't be a fool, Kathy. It's too dangerous for you to try to leave."

It was just as dangerous for her to stay! "Dammit, I'm not afraid of a swift river," she said aloud. "I've been white-water rafting on the Nahanni, for heaven's sake!"

"Sorry," he said, sounding not at all apologetic. "No raft, no boat, nothing but Art's old canoe out in the shed and that leaks too much. We're cut off. The hill has become an island, and most of town is underwater to one degree or another."

Kathy returned to the table and sank into her chair. "But . . ." She bit her lip, looking instinctively to Gabe for reassurance. Old habits die hard.

"Not our place," she almost pleaded. "It's halfway up the hill!"

"That's right, it is, and it's probably not flooded. But it's halfway up the hill on the other side of the river, I might remind you, in case you're thinking of doing something stupid like walking out of here when I've gone to sleep."

"Dammit, Gabe, I wouldn't do such a stupid thing, but I'm not so sure about my father. If I know Mike, he's busting his back, risking his life to get every little story, every possible photograph. And if the office—and even our house—is underwater, he's set up a darkroom somewhere else, has a typewriter perched on somebody's desk, and is determined to get out Thursday's edition even if he has to hand-crank an ancient press to do it. He needs me."

Gabe wanted to say, *He can't have you, I need you more*, but bit the words off before they could form. He reached across the table and took one of her icy hands. Lord, would she ever get warm again? He knew he could warm her, wanted to do it so badly it hurt, but he wouldn't. Not if he could help it. "I know he does, and I know how much you want to see him. I promise I'll get you there just as soon as I can. Just don't . . . don't act as if you're afraid to stay here with me."

Kathy felt the warmth of his skin, the hardness of it, the strength of his fingers and was torn between wanting to curl her hand around his and wanting to jerk free and run. Oh, but she was afraid all right, though not of him. And it was such a delicious, thrilling fear that she wanted it to go on curling through her, exciting her, making her blood run hotter and hotter and . . .

"If you don't quit looking at me like that, you might just have something to be afraid of after all," he said in a softly warning tone.

"Gabe . . ." Her voice was little more than a whisper. "I've never been afraid of you. Not before, not now, not ever."

Three

"You should be afraid," he said, rubbing a thumb over her knuckles, his gaze locked on hers. "Because I am. We can't both live here, you know. They won't leave us alone."

"They?"

"The community. The biddies. Do you know what it's been like these past few years? Hearing from all of them over and over again what *you've* been doing, where you've been working, how successful you're becoming? Having magazines shoved in my face so I can see your byline, your photographs, your immortal words? Seeing the censure in their eyes, knowing each one of them finds it unforgivable that I went away and left my childhood sweetheart with a broken heart. They want me to suffer, knowing you're doing fine without me."

"Hey, come on. They don't matter. They—"

"They all adored you," he went on as if she hadn't spoken. "And blamed me. Of course, they were right, but they'd have blamed me just as much if I'd done what I wanted to do then and you'd gotten pregnant. They don't seem to think about the fact that at seventeen you were still a child in many ways, but as a man of twenty-two, I wasn't."

"Gabriel . . . *I* thought of it. Later. I know that what you did, leaving the way you did, was the only choice you had. And don't forget, I chose to leave too. And I'm glad I did."

"Then choose to leave again, Kathy. Please! Don't think about living here. Don't let yourself be trapped."

"I have thought about it," she said, "and my choice is to stay. I don't think it's going to feel like a trap anymore. Every woman needs a home eventually. I think it's time I made one for myself, and not just an apartment in a Toronto high rise that I see once every three or four months. I need a real home and work that lets me stay near it. It's all I've dreamed about for the last several years."

He paled. "Kathy—"

"No," she said quickly, pulling her hand out from under his and shoving her chair back as she got to her feet. "Don't say anything. I didn't mean it like that."

What could he do, apologize as he had fourteen years ago, as he hadn't four years ago but surely would have if she'd hung around long enough to give him the chance? "I'm not going to get in your way, Gabe, or expect anything from you. That's all in the past now, and we're better off leaving it there." She picked up their dishes and stacked them, carrying them to the sink. "There's no need to talk about it."

He watched her from his chair at the table. "We have to talk about it. It's there between us, only now because we have loved each other, it's worse."

It was. She recognized that too. The memory of their having made love caused a pulsing ache inside her that she couldn't ignore, and each time she saw the same desire in his eyes, it increased hers. Still, as she turned to face him she said musingly, "We should have learned something from what happened during that cruise. I thought I had learned."

"What did you think you'd learned, Kath?"

Not to believe that love could make everything right, not to trust, not to have faith. Neither love nor trust nor faith brought her what she'd hoped for. It had all, in the end, been false. In spite of her sadness, she managed a smile. "That what we once shared was an illusion, just as our one night together proved to be an illusion."

"It didn't feel like that at the time, honey. And maybe illusion is the wrong word. What about 'delusion'?" He smiled, just a brief twisting of his lips that was perhaps more of a grimace. "But even a pragmatic man can still cling to the odd delusion," he added, more to himself than to her.

And so could a pragmatic woman. It would be so easy to delude herself, to let herself believe that maybe there was a chance. All she had to do was walk back to where he sat and say a fervent and heartfelt yes! to the silent plea in his eyes. Instead, she said, "I have none at all."

"You're deluding yourself if you think we can relegate what we feel to the past, Kathy." He got to his feet and walked slowly toward her. She turned away, gripping the edge of the sink. "This is the present, and you know as well as I do that nothing basic has changed between us, and if you stay . . ." He came up behind her, slipped his arms around her, and drew her back against him. She remained stiff and unyielding in his embrace.

"Everything has changed between us," she replied evenly.

He turned her and looked into her eyes. "You're right, of course. It changed the night we made love together." He felt her body's involuntary quiver in reaction to his words. Part of him exulted over her response, and he went on. "Before I left here, your feelings were those of a girl. The next time we met, they were the feelings of a mature woman. And they still are." He cupped her chin in one hand. "Aren't they?"

"Don't," she said, placing a hand on his chest to hold him away, nearly choked by the rising need to feel his lips on hers just one more time. They were close, so close she could see a small split in his lower lip. She wanted to reach up and rub her fingertip over it, soothe it, or press her own lips to it. Had he bit it in fear when he realized who it was on the roof of that car?

"Don't what?"

"Don't hold me like this. Don't . . . kiss me," she added when his mouth descended purposefully toward hers.

"I have to," he murmured, and she sighed, her breath mingling with his, feeling the warmth of his lips as they brushed over hers, the wet tip of his tongue as he sought the entry she denied him.

"Open your mouth," he said after a moment, lifting his lips from hers only a fraction of an inch. "Do I have to teach you all over again how to kiss?"

"No . . ." Was she answering his question or protesting? If it was a protest, it was the weakest one she had ever made, because somehow her mouth had parted and his tongue was drawing a tingling line across the inside of her bottom lip. Then, with a groan that could have come from either of them, they clung to each other, rocking together, mouths locked, bodies pressed tightly together as waves of delight and gratitude and desire swept through them. Kathy felt the hardness of his body, the tremor in his hands, the strength of his arms. His hair was crisp and cool, the skin of his neck warm, satiny. And his mouth, his tongue, hot and sweet and wet. With all her heart, she welcomed his kiss and returned it with passion that knew no end.

"Mine," he said moments later, his hands around her head, his lips moving over her uptilted face, his eyes only half-open. "Mine."

"No," she said. "Don't say that. It isn't true."

"You are mine. You've always been mine." He kissed her eyes closed, kissed her earlobes, kissed her mouth again and again. "I need you. Come with me. Let me love you again." His breath whispered over her face, over her neck, into the parted lapels of the red robe she wore. His day's growth of beard was deliciously harsh against her soft skin, and she moved against him even while she struggled to force herself to move away. "Kathy, now . . ." He shifted his hold on her, half-bending to scoop her off her feet.

"No!" she said again, and this time she meant it. "No, Gabriel. Don't." She wasn't his. She wouldn't be his again, because he could never really be hers. "Stop. Let me go." She pushed against his chest, and he stepped back half a pace, still keeping his arms loosely around her. His eyes were full of need— and resignation—his chest rose and fell rapidly as he shuddered. Then he closed his eyes tightly before breaking free completely.

"Okay," he said. "Okay. Sorry." He gripped the top of the refrigerator, head hanging down between his strong arms. Slowly, he regained control of his breathing. She saw his throat work as he swallowed. He lifted his head finally and looked at her. "It's too soon. I know."

"It's not just too soon. It's . . . not going to happen. I didn't come back here for this. I didn't even know you'd be here."

He walked away, but she could still feel the heat of his body. "And if you had?" he asked intensely. "Would you still have decided to come?"

She met his burning gaze, cooled it with her words. "For Mike's sake, yes, I'd have decided to come. Just as, for his sake, I intend to stay, and for my own sake, I intend to stay away from you."

He looked at her bleakly for several moments, then nodded. That wasn't going to be possible, for either of them, and she knew it as well as he did. But Kathy had always been stubborn. He wouldn't even try to convince her. Events were bound to do that for him. "I made up Mom's room for you when you were in the bath. I have to be out early in the morning. Good night, Kathy."

"Good night," she said, but doubted if he heard her. She stood where she was, listening to his feet thudding dully as he mounted the carpeted stairs. Then, with a sigh, she turned out the lights in the kitchen and hall, opened the door to Grace Fowler's room, and stepped inside, looking with sudden longing at the big bed under its green flowered canopy. She knew she wouldn't sleep, but, oh, how she needed rest!

The last thing she thought as she rolled to her side and tugged up the covers was that if Gabe was going to be out early in the morning, then so would she . . .

It seemed while the thought to leave with Gabe was still forming in her mind, she heard the rattle of a helicopter coming in to land and opened her eyes to daylight.

Why she suspected he would leave without her she didn't know, but before she could give it any thought, she was on her feet, snatching the red robe around herself and tearing out the door. "Gabriel! You wait for me!" she cried, flinging herself against the kitchen door he was trying to open.

"Sorry," he said, picking her up and setting her aside. "There's no time."

"It will take me thirty seconds to dress," she insisted, clutching two fistfuls of flying suit in her hands and possibly, judging from the pained look on his face, a few chest hairs as well. She didn't care. He shifted, gripping her wrists, trying to break free of her hold, but she refused to let go. "Just wait, Gabe. Give me a minute. You can drop me off down below before you go about your business."

"Kathy, we can't! That helicopter is needed for important rescue work, and you don't need to be rescued."

"I need to get off this hilltop," she argued. "I have to get home to my dad."

"Listen to me! I promised I'd get you to Mike as soon as I could, but today it's not possible. The rain is still coming down. The river is still rising. There are people in danger. Little children, animals. Think about that! There isn't time to cater to a scared little girl who simply wants her daddy!"

"Damn you!" she exploded. "You know it's not like that! And look at all the time you're wasting arguing with me! I could have been dressed and in that helicopter by now and—"

The door beside them thundered under the force of the fist banging on its other side. Gabe, holding her wrists in one hand, flung it open.

"Let's go, let's go," said a tall man, also dressed in orange. "Come on, Fowler, snap it up. We haven't got all—" When he saw Kathy, red robe awry, hair in spikes, face flushed with anger, he said, "Oh. Sorry. I'll wait outside, but get a move on."

"Wait, no, it's not what—" Kathy began, and broke off in frustration as the man slammed the door. "Dammit," she said. "Tell him to wait for me!"

"Not a chance," said Gabe, still holding her wrists.

He let one go, swung her hard against him, and kissed her for one wild, head-spinning moment. Then he was out the door. She was right on his heels, down the steps, shouting after him, but the hem of the robe tripped her up, and she fell facefirst into the wet grass. Before she could begin to collect herself, she heard the note of the chopper's engine change, and by the time she was running again, through the curtain of rain which fell unrelentingly, the aircraft was several feet above the ground and rising fast.

"If you really believe it's that easy," she shouted after it, "I've got a big surprise for you, Fowler!" Come hell or high water, she would get off this farm, and she would do it that day.

It was, of course, the high water that stopped her. When she saw the brown swill swirling around the toes of her wet pink sneakers, stretching away into the gloom of rain, nothing but drowned trees on the far side, she knew she was stopped—but only temporarily. Gritting her teeth, she trudged back up the long, winding hill to the farm. Gabe wasn't as smart as he thought he was. Had he forgotten he'd mentioned that leaky canoe? She found it in the woodshed, and it might have done, only she saw at once that the canoe was more than just leaky. Someone had used an axe on its bottom. She picked up the axe lying there and swung it hard, setting its blade into the chopping block, wrenching it out and swinging it all over again. *Damn the man! Damn him! And damn him again!*

Kathy was a lot warmer and a lot drier, but no less angry when she heard the helicopter returning. This time she was halfway across the field before it had finished discharging its load of passengers. All children, she realized. Gabe met her, his long strides eating up the distance between them. He thrust a warm, soft bundle into her arms.

"What—" she began, but he cut her off by bending and placing a hot kiss firmly on her mouth.

She jerked her mouth free. "Dammit!"

The bundle in her arms squirmed, and she looked down at a tiny, wrinkled face, all screwed up to cry because the rain was falling on it. Instinctively, she cuddled it closer, protecting it, and, with a grin, Gabe said, "Special delivery, just for you. More to come. You'll find everything you need stored in the basement. See you in a bit."

"Gabriel!" She started to go after him, but a small child clutched her around the knees, and she came close to landing on the wet grass again. Somehow she caught her balance but once more had to stand and watch her only means of getting off the hill claw its way into the sky.

At the roar of the helicopter, the child clutching her knees screamed in terror, and she crouched down to gather her close in her free arm. "Hey, come on, little one. It's okay. There's nothing to be afraid of. There, now, let Kathy pick you up too. You're not much more than a baby, are you?"

Standing, she lifted the toddler along with the infant, and said, "Are you hungry?" addressing the question not only to the weeping child who leaned on her shoulder but also to the other five, all of whom were huddled together not far away. "Come on in, kids," she said, over the noise the crying child made. "Let's get out of the rain."

They followed her obediently onto the porch, but there most of them stopped. One little girl took a step closer, but the other four stoically remained where they were.

"Come on," she said again. "We'll get some lunch

going. I bet you're all starving." She smiled at the one who had taken that step. "What's your name?"

The child looked blank. Kathy frowned, focusing on the other children as well. There was something strange about their mode of dress. They almost looked like refugees from the set of *Little House on the Prairie*. The boys wore thickly woven pants, beautifully hand-knit sweaters under their wet coats and jackets, and heavy boots. The girls wore dark stockings sticking out from under longish skirts, and one—the eldest—had a small white cap on her head. Were they from some kind of children's home, or something? And their silence made her uncomfortable. They were watchful, wary, suspicious.

Were they handicapped in some way? Maybe deaf? Maybe retarded? They certainly could be either with their lack of response to her suggestion of food. Setting the toddler down just inside the kitchen, she reached out and took the little girl's hand.

She was met with resistance, resistance that increased when one of the other children—the biggest by far, though he couldn't have been more than ten—said sternly, *"Marta, nein!"*

"Oh, my Lord!" Kathy said. "I don't believe this! That inconsiderate, unspeakable man flies in here, kisses me so I can't think, and then puts me in charge of children who don't even speak my language? I'm going to kill him! At the very least!"

One of the older children spoke again, and again the language was German. Kathy groaned. Oh, heavens! What were they? Hutterite? Mennonite? Of course. That explained the little white cap on the biggest girl. Did any of them speak English? And if not, was her particular brand of German good enough for them to understand her? Clearly, they were cold and wet and likely traumatized from having been put into a helicopter.

Poor little mites. She smiled at them, offered them bread and cheese in her best German, which was, she feared, not all that great. But they must have understood her, because Marta ceased resisting. As if that were the signal they'd been waiting for, the rest of the children followed, the older two coming in only just enough so that Kathy could shut the door. Then standing there, flanking it, as if on guard, they glared at the other children, but mostly, Kathy noted, at her. What was it, anyway? Did she look like an axe-murderer? With a guilty pang, she remembered her thoughts about that axe in the woodshed. Maybe they were justified in fearing her.

She gave them a tentative smile that was not returned, and set about preparing lunch with one child cradled in her left arm and another one clinging to her right knee. When the larger children were all settled at the table, she managed to find a safe place to put the infant. About to go into the basement to find the things Gabe had said would be there to help her with this venture into foster parenting, she heard the helicopter circling low over the house once more. What had he said? More to come? Oh, no! No. She had plenty to handle with this batch! She lunged at the door and swung it open just as the aircraft settled onto the grass again.

"Oh, no you don't!" she shouted, leaping off the back porch, feeling the wetness soak into her socks as Gabe came toward her carrying not one, but two bundles. And he was followed by several more small, wet figures. "Listen, Noah," she said. "You find somebody else to paddle your damned ark!"

"Kathy, there *isn't* anyone else!"

She gritted her teeth in frustration. "Gabriel Fowler, do you know that those kids don't speak a word of English?"

"Neither do these," he said, depositing the two bundles in her arms. "But that doesn't make them any less children, does it? Besides, I have a distinct recollection of your speaking German to a certain Austrian ski bum. You'll manage." He reached into one of the pockets in his flying suit and withdrew two baby bottles full of milk, tucking them between her arm and her chest. "I need your help, Kath. Don't fight me on this."

"Gabe! Dammit . . ." she began, wanting to tell him that the German she had practiced on Dieter wasn't good enough under these circumstances. Then she realized he was right. She couldn't fight him. They were just children, no matter what language they spoke. It would have been pointless to go on, anyway, because Gabe had turned from her and was leaving.

She had to smile. When had anyone, least of all her, been able to refuse Gabriel Fowler anything?

As she walked back to the house, her step was light. It might not have been the way she would have chosen to help with the rescue effort, but it was something she was able to do, capable of doing, and so she would do it.

As the helicopter disappeared behind a ridge, Kathy turned away and smiled at the five newcomers, who all looked bewildered and wet and cold. *"Kommt, Kinder,"* she said gently. *"Kommt aus dem Regen."*

Many hours later, when the helicopter buzzed the house before landing with its customary clatter on the wet grass, Kathy's stomach fluttered—try as she did to pretend that it hadn't—and she went outside just as eagerly as Hans, the taciturn ten-year-old who had stood waiting by the door most of the afternoon. He pulled his jacket tighter around him and bolted out ahead of her. Pausing on the porch just long enough to shove her feet into her shoes, Kathy saw the boy hurtle across the yard to be caught by an orange-suited figure who intercepted his headlong dash toward the lifting aircraft.

"Stop it! Settle down!" she heard Gabe say as he held Hans back so that the boy's hard boots couldn't make contact with his shins. "If you have so much energy, there are a couple of cows in the barn that need milking."

"Nein! Nein! Ich—"

"Hans!" Kathy grabbed the angry boy from behind to pull him back from Gabe, but somehow, as Gabe moved, she ended up drawn tightly against his side, as they both held onto the boy. Hans tore free and took off running, coming to a halt where the marks of the helicopter's skids still depressed the grass, his face lifted to the darkening sky as if willing the chopper to return.

"Son," said Gabe, approaching him. "This is where your father wants you to be. You know that. It's best. Now, will you milk for me? He said you were the best of all the boys at doing that."

Hans looked both rebellious and grief-stricken, then nodded and, head down, plodded toward the barn and disappeared from sight.

"Poor kid," said Gabe, and Kathy saw with a pang that his face was drawn with fatigue. He didn't need this on top of whatever kind of bad day he'd had. "The other kids his age are filling sandbags like an assembly line crew, but Hans has a serious heart murmur. His father . . ." His voice trailed away in a sigh.

"I'm sorry," she said. "I knew his state of mind. I should have been quicker and kept him inside. Let me go and I'll try to talk some sense into him. His sister says he speaks English, but so far today he's

refused to respond to it. Not that he answers me
when I speak German, either, but maybe this time
he will."

"No," Gabe said, tightening his hold on her, pulling her toward the porch. "He's out there crying,
and for that he needs privacy. Besides, obedience is
something trained into those kids from birth. While
he cries, he'll milk the cows."

"You said 'a couple of cows'?"

"That's right. Just enough milk for us and whatever range orphans I have to raise," Gabe said, leading her back toward the house.

"But . . . You're not dairy farming?"

He shook his head and mounted the steps. "No."
His one word closed the subject. On the porch, still
with an arm around her, Gabe came to a halt and
looked down at her. He smiled as if with relief that
she was still all in one piece, still there, as he added,
"I sort of thought you might have run away."

She stepped out of his loose embrace, tilting her
face up toward him. "Really? How? The canoe seems
to have met with an accident."

His face darkened momentarily. "So you did try."

Something flared in her. Was it hope? Was it joy?
Dammit, why did she keep on diligently searching
for tiny bits of proof that he cared about her, that
his feelings for her were more than just physical?
Because she was in no doubt about that aspect of
his feelings, she told herself angrily. And because,
fool that she was, she wanted more and kept on
hoping that somewhere, in spite of all evidence to
the contrary, it existed.

"You knew I'd try. Or have you forgotten that much
about me?"

After a moment, Gabe smiled slowly and wiped
beads of rain from her face. "I knew you'd try," he
said. "I haven't forgotten one solitary thing about

you." His smile faded. "I had to stop you. I had to be sure you were safe. Have you forgotten that much about me?"

"No." She looked into his eyes, wondering if he had been as strongly protective of his wife. Of course he had. She let herself think for a moment what it must have been like for that woman to carry Gabe's child. His wife, she was certain, would have needed a strong and determined personality in order not to have been completely smothered with care during her pregnancy. She would have needed to be a woman much like Kathy M'Gonigle, unwilling, maybe even unable, to back down from a fight or to be walked on.

Except, Kathy had backed down, hadn't she? She had done more than that—she'd left Gabe, walked away from the most important fight of her life four years ago, without ever giving herself a chance—or him. Suddenly, the heavy thoughts that had overwhelmed her the previous night became lighter, clearer, and a glimmer of a notion began to grow. She stared at him speculatively. What if she were to fight for what she knew she and Gabe could have? What were her chances of winning?

"What's wrong?"

She shook her head, allowing her smile to shine through, wondering if it showed all the sudden triumph she was feeling. "Nothing. Come on. Let's go inside."

Gabe nodded and pulled her deep into the circle of his arms. "What's that smile for?" He grasped a handful of her hair and tipped her head back.

"Happiness."

He looked awed. "Lord! What would it take to make you look that happy all the time?"

She could have told him but didn't. That was something he was going to have to figure out for himself. Of course, she wasn't averse to lending a sneaky bit of help here and there if his cognitive abilities had rusted over the years. But all she said was, "I've enjoyed today."

"Good." He drew her an inch closer. "Did I say thanks for taking the kids in for me?"

Her stomach fluttered again. "No, but I have a feeling you're about to."

"Yeah," he said, bending his head to cover her mouth with his own, his lips moving seductively over hers. "Kathy . . ." he sighed against her lips several sweet moments later. "Oh, babe . . . This is crazy, but sweet, so sweet."

"I know." She didn't try to get away. "I've always had my doubts about your sanity."

"Um-hmm," he agreed, and his mouth hardened over hers, as he kissed her with such depth of feeling that tears rose into her eyes, and her chest ached with the strength of her emotions. He couldn't kiss her like that if he was still in love with his wife. She had been so wrong to think that if he had loved another woman it meant he couldn't love her. If he was capable of loving someone else, then he was capable of giving her exactly the same, and somehow, she was going to have to make him aware of that.

"Go ahead," she said. "Live dangerously. Be crazy. Kiss me again."

"Crazy it may be, but it's so very, very necessary that I don't think I can quit," he whispered when he lifted his head. "I never thought I could be so tired one minute and so energized the next. You feed something inside me, Kathy M'Gonigle, and yet I get hungrier and hungrier each time I see you. What are we going to do about it?"

"Feed you some more," she murmured, pulling his head down and kissing him with the same kind of deep longing with which he had kissed her. "And me too."

Four

"Stop, Kathy," Gabe said, gasping when he could stand no more of her torment. He pulled away from her to lean on the wall and run a hand through his wet hair. He looked at her parted lips, lifted one hand, and ran a thumb over them. "It feels so damned good to hold you."

She managed a wobbly smile. He must know the feeling was mutual. He'd always known that about her. She didn't have to tell him. Instead, she said, "Come on in. You must be starving. Dinner's nearly ready."

If it didn't cross her mind how much like a wife she sounded in that moment, it did, however, strike Gabe. He stood there just outside the door looking in at her standing in the glow of the lights, and he ached with a yearning so strong, he nearly groaned aloud with it.

She smiled quizzically at him, silently asking why he wasn't coming inside, and he drew in a deep breath before stepping over the threshold into the warmth of the big kitchen, where the air was redolent of spaghetti sauce. Gabe felt his heart fill, dispelling the aching void of yearning. He put his arm around Kathy's shoulder again and just stood there, drawing in the sights and scents and sounds of the room, and the feel of the woman at his side.

This was the way it should be. A man should come home to a warm kitchen filled with good smells, and a warm woman who ran to his arms and comforted him.

He knew it wasn't always that way these days, that a man was just as likely to come home to do the cooking and be waiting with a warm embrace for his woman when she came in the door. That would be good, too, but he could dream, couldn't he? He turned his head and looked down at Kathy. Oh, yes, every now and then it didn't hurt to dream, as long as he didn't let the dreams overshadow reality.

With the hand that had been cupping the tip of her shoulder, Gabe nudged her face up. "You're nice to come home to," he murmured, and dropped another kiss onto her lips, this time just a light one, a casual one, as if the kisses they had exchanged on the porch had existed in another time or place—or not at all, Kathy thought.

"Cupboard love." She pulled away from him without responding beyond a flare in her eyes that he suspected she couldn't suppress, and said, "We aren't alone, you know."

"I did know that," he said, and glanced across the room toward where Giesela, the eleven-year-old, in her little white cap and her old-fashioned dress, stood contentedly stirring the contents of the big pot. She smiled shyly at Gabe and Kathy, then looked down into the steam, a rosy-cheeked anachronism that prompted Gabe to say, "I feel as if I've just stepped back into the last century. Where are the others?"

Kathy gave him a guilty grin. "In the den, I'm

sorry to say. Having a wonderful time being introduced to the pleasurable sins of this century. Hans was most disapproving, and Giesela refused politely but firmly, but believe me, your VCR, Bambi, and Bugs Bunny have really saved my day!"

Gabe shouted with laughter. "Oh, my Lord! And I assured those good people their children would be safe here! Now what am I going to tell them?"

Kathy shook her head and shrugged, laughing with him. "I don't know. But I'm sure you'll think of something, and if you can't, you can lay the blame on me."

Then, sobering, she added, "And I will tell them that their children were kept warm and safe and . . . loved, and if that wasn't good enough, then I'm sorry."

Gabe touched her cheek. "That's all any parent could ask for," he said softly, and she wondered if he'd had a chance to see his own son during the day or whether he had spent all his time making sure other people's children were safe and well cared for. As she had ever since he'd told her about his son, she experienced a pang, thinking about Gabe as a father—and somebody else's husband.

As several of the children came out of the den, and Gabe crouched to speak to them, she saw the genuine caring in his face. Oh, yes, he loved children, just as she'd always thought he would. But why . . . why wasn't it *her* children he came home to? A spasm of grief twisted inside her, but she forced it down, watching a little girl giggle and squirm then shriek with laughter as Gabe tossed her high in the air. The other small ones waited their turns, some shyly, some impatiently, but all received a share of his attention. The older ones, who had learned some English, gave him a report on their day, and Kathy was pleased and surprised to learn that they had enjoyed her songs and piano playing as much as they had watching Bambi and the other movies.

As she turned on the heat under the large pot of water she had ready for boiling spaghetti, Gabe set the last child down and got to his feet, pulling two more baby bottles out of one of his pockets. "Here we go. More mama's milk for the babies." He stood close to her as he opened the refrigerator.

" 'Mama's milk'?" Kathy stared aghast at Gabe. "I didn't know that was breast milk you brought earlier! I ran out, and I've been feeding those babies cows' milk! Will it hurt them?"

He scratched his head. "How do I know? You're the woman around here. Babies drink cows' milk all the time, don't they? That's what Ricky had."

"Well, you're the parent! Didn't . . ." She frowned. She didn't even know his wife's name. "Didn't Ricky's mother breast feed him?"

His face took on a closed look. "No."

Unzipping his flying suit, he leaned on the high chair in the corner and tugged off one of his boots. "I guess it was a good thing Mom insisted I keep all Ricky's baby junk."

"That's not junk. They're treasures!" she declared, stirring several handfuls of spaghetti into the boiling water. "At least to me they are." Then, changing the subject: "You have time to shower before dinner, if you want. Should it take Hans long to finish milking?"

"I'll go give him a hand, then shower," said Gabe, heading for the door again, slinging a yellow raincoat over his shoulders. "Go ahead with dinner, though. By the time it's ready, we'll be ready too."

"Gabe!" The protest was out before she could stop it. He turned, his brows raised in question, his head tilted to a slight angle.

"I—" She drew a deep breath. It wasn't her business. Nor was it her place to tell him what to do, but . . . "Dammit, you're beat. You shouldn't go out again."

He smiled, and her insides did their crazy tricks again. "You're beat too," he said quietly. "I don't notice you stopping." She shrugged, suddenly distinctly uncomfortable under his scrutiny. "I won't be long," he said, and went out.

"I'm sorry I had to do this to you," Gabe said hours later from his sprawled position on the living room couch. The house was dim and quiet. All the children slept. "But there didn't seem to be any other solution. Those people were trying so hard to build up their dikes, and they needed all hands, even the mothers of young children. And the kids needed to be somewhere safe, just in case the dikes didn't hold. I remembered that you spoke some German, so I persuaded the families that you were the best choice, and that up here, the kids would all be fine. You did retain what German you knew, didn't you?"

"Yes, not that it was very much. But surprisingly, I found it coming back."

He sighed and leaned back, his head resting on the back of the sofa, and Kathy knew without being told that he was remembering when he had first learned that she spoke some German, remembering the tall, blond passenger who had danced constant attendance on her for all but the last night of her voyage on the *Orion*.

"Why don't you go to bed?" she suggested. He rolled his head sideways and looked at her again.

"With whom?" he asked with a wry grin. For a moment, she thought he was being cute, but then she remembered that all the beds, the couches, the floor in the den, and part of the upstairs hallway were covered with pallets and sleeping bags and blankets and softly breathing small bodies.

She smiled. "Right where you are looks pretty good to me. I bet if I gave you a shove, you'd fall over sideways and not move until morning."

He yawned once more and nodded. "Don't try it. You're probably right, and this is where I intend for you to sleep."

"I think I can squeeze in beside Giesela and Marta in your mother's bed. Neither one of them is very big." As she got to her feet, Gabe rose, too, and stood close to her, his hands encircling her ribs just below her breasts.

"Neither are you." His fingers moved as if feeling the bones barely covered by her flesh and skin. "We could share that couch."

She looked up into his eyes, feeling the warmth of his gaze, the strength of his hands on her, and wanted, with a longing so intense she didn't know how she withstood it, to move into his embrace as she had on the porch. But then there had been a houseful of children to contend with. The children still existed, but she didn't think her control would if she permitted herself to hold Gabe, to be held by him. So she wouldn't. Making love with him was not part of her plan. At least not yet. First, she wanted his love—then would come the lovemaking.

"Not a chance, Fowler."

He grinned. "One can but try." Then, on a complete change of subject, he said, "I'm glad you were here for those children, Kathy."

"So am I. You know I couldn't turn down little kids in need."

He gazed at her, slipping one hand down to her waist, and lifting the other to stroke a finger down the side of her face. His touch sent a shiver down her spine and a puckering thrill to her nipples. "Yes, I know that," he said after a moment. "Dammit, I knew that, Kath, and so I used you. It wasn't exactly fair, was it?"

"It's okay. You know I love children." Her voice was jerky, her palms damp as she clenched her fists at her sides, determined not to let him see her reactions to him, determined not to let herself give in to them.

"Yes. Oh, hell, that's what makes this all so damned difficult. I had no right to keep you here, no right to—" He broke off, misery in his eyes. Then, while she stood and lost herself in his gaze, attempting to decipher what he meant, he drew her impatiently against his body.

"I have no right to do this, either, do I?" he asked, stroking his hands down her back to her hips, cupping her buttocks, and drawing her to his hardness.

"But right and wrong seem to lose their sharp edges when you're this close to me."

"Wrong?" she asked, her heart pounding slowly and heavily in her chest. "Where does the 'wrong' come in, Gabriel?" It was herself she should be putting that question to, she knew, but his closeness was robbing her of good sense, good intentions, everything but the need to be closer.

"It's wrong for you," he murmured, burrowing his mouth against her neck for a moment before lifting his head. "And for once in my life, I'd like not to hurt you, not to do the wrong thing where you're concerned. I should have taken you to your dad as soon as I picked you up. Bringing you here was a mistake."

His words stung her, and her flimsy hopes began to wither away. Was she out of her mind believing that her love for him was strong enough to overcome all the obstacles he kept erecting? Earlier, it had seemed so clear, so simple; she loved him. She was strong. She would fight for him in every way possible and not give up until she had what she wanted—his ring on her finger. His love in her heart.

"A mistake for whom?"

"For me. For you. For . . . everyone concerned."

She felt suddenly chilled in spite of his closeness. Of course. Everyone concerned. There were more than just herself and Gabe to be considered. There was still his wife, even though she was an ex-wife. She was an unknown factor, and even while Kathy told herself that Gabe couldn't want her the way he did if he still loved someone else, she felt doubts creeping back. And then there was his son. Maybe Gabe had every intention of raising his son alone. Could that be what he preferred? After all, two could make a family just the same as three or four. She and her father had been a family of two for almost as long as she could remember. Of course, Gabe had his mother too. He had said he was running the farm for her and . . .

"Gabriel." Her brows drew together, and she pushed out of his embrace. "Tell me why you're here, really. You said this isn't a dairy farm anymore, yet Art turned it into one years ago and . . . Where *is* Art?"

She thought for a few moments that he wasn't going to answer. He went back to the couch and sat down, burying his face in his hands. Then, lifting his head, he said bluntly, "Art's in . . . a hospital, Kath. At least, they call it that. But then they go and wreck it by adding the words 'maximum security'. It's a prison. He's there for murder."

"Oh, no . . ."

It was only a tiny thread of sound. She shook her head, unable to believe what she knew must be true. If it weren't so, Gabe wouldn't have said it, but it was such a horrific thought, she wanted to deny it.

Art had been a bully. He had made Gabe's youth miserable. He had made a lot of people's youths miserable. But murder? Impulsively, she crouched before Gabe and took his hands in her own. His were icy cold, slightly damp. His face was drawn. "Tell me about it," she said softly.

"He killed a young couple who were camping in the hills over to the east. No one knows why he did . . . what he did. I guess we'll never know, except that he was completely crazy. No sane person could have done . . . those things. He wouldn't admit it, even when . . . when . . . an eyewitness came forward to say that he'd been seen in the area at the time of the killings. Then, when the police checked, his fingerprints were found all over their camper and his sperm—" Gabe broke off, shuddering. He jerked free of her and dropped his face to his hands again, and his shoulders heaved just once.

"Gabe. Don't. It's all right. I'm sorry. I shouldn't have asked. Don't talk about it anymore." She sat on the arm of the sofa and stroked his neck with one hand. Presently, he lifted his head to look at her.

"You should know about it."

Kathy shook her head. "You don't need to tell me."

He looked at her bleakly. "Why not? The minute you hit the village, everyone else will." But oh, Lord, he wished her father had told her instead of leaving it for him to do. Why had Mike kept it from her? Because of his own involvement, or because he didn't want her to know that Gabriel was living in the valley again?

"Gabe, I don't listen to gossip."

"This isn't gossip. This is the truth." Pulling in a deep breath, he leaned forward, hands braced on the edge of the sofa as if he might leap up at any moment. "And I'd rather have you hear the truth from me than speculation from other people. Not that the rumors could be any worse than the truth, when it comes right down to it.

"He didn't just murder that young couple," he went on in a harsh tone, sparing her nothing—nor himself. "He raped the woman, then killed both of them and . . . mutilated their bodies. The details were all over the papers before he was arrested and charged. The guy who found them was too shocked and horrified to keep quiet about what he'd seen, and it was printed in the newspapers in gruesome detail."

She felt sick. "Not Dad's?" As good a newsman as her father was, as much as he believed in writing the truth, she couldn't believe he would print something so terrible. He'd think of the victims' families.

"No. The city papers. The police weren't happy about it, but it was done before they could get a court order to stop it."

Kathy closed her eyes briefly, shaking her head. "Oh, Gabe! What a terrible thing."

"Art was found to be criminally insane and will probably never be released. Not unless they think he's cured, and that kind of insanity never is, is it?"

"No. I don't think so." Her eyes filled with tears she tried to blink away, but they only spilled over onto her cheeks.

Gabe reached up and brushed them away. "For Art?" he asked, incredulous.

She shook her head. "No, not for him. Oh, partly, maybe. I don't know. I haven't had a chance to think about it yet. What he did was monstrous, but like you said, he did it because he was totally insane. I guess I'm thinking of his victims and their families, but mostly your poor mother. And you and Rachel."

Although Art was Grace Fowler's stepson, she had loved him as much as she had her two younger children. Gabe had once told her that when he was a child, he'd thought his mother loved Art a lot more than she did either him or Rachel. As an adult, though, he'd realized she'd bent over backward to make her difficult stepson feel loved and wanted.

Gabe nodded. Kathy didn't know the half of it, and that, for sure, was something he wasn't about to tell her. "We all suffered. Rachel wanted to break her engagement to Graham, but he insisted the wedding go on as planned. It was the best thing he could have done for her, because he's with the forestry service down on the coast. It got her out of here during the worst of it—the trial, the bad publicity, all that. It was a rough time. But especially for Mom. She felt she was to blame, of course, even though everyone assured her that she wasn't."

No, he thought, Grace wasn't to blame. He was. Gabriel. Gabriel the coward who could have prevented all this from happening if he'd only had the courage to tell his mother, tell the police, tell someone, anyone, that his own father's death might not have been the accident they'd all believed it to be. He was guilty of silence, guilty of letting Art get away with murder—his own father's murder—and nothing would ever change that. He shuddered. Art might be in one kind of prison, but the one he was in had even stronger walls.

"Rachel and I both wanted Mom to get out of the valley, but she wouldn't," he went on. "Yeah, it was rough on her, all right."

"And you."

He shrugged. "And me. It's not easy being known as the brother of a crazed murderer, watching people watching me, wondering if the same germ of insanity lurks in my brain."

"No one who knows you would even consider it!" She was aghast at the idea that any of the neighbors would think such a thing. Or that he would suspect it of them. "Come on, Gabe, Art was always . . . different. You've told me that yourself. And you certainly weren't the only one to feel that way. I remember when we were teenagers, the other kids felt sorry for Rachel because she had such a strange older brother."

His grin was wry. "Maybe they meant me."

"Idiot! You were away at college."

In truth, their friends had used the term "weird" and had expressed horror at the thought of her going into the home of that "awful man," even if she was going there with his very normal sister and, when Gabe was home from college, with his perfectly wonderful younger brother.

"I know what people always said about Art." He sighed again, looking at her from under half-shuttered lids. "And they—we—were right."

"I know it bothered you to have people talking about him," she said. "Even though—" She broke off abruptly and looked down, not wanting to finish the sentence.

"Even though I hated him? It's okay to say it. I never tried to hide that from you. But, strangely, I don't hate him anymore. This changed things in some way. Now I only pity him. I wish—" he broke off, running a hand through his hair and shaking his head. "I don't condone what he did, but I'm sorry for him. Can you understand that?"

She nodded. It was odd, but she did understand in a way and shared a little of Gabe's pity for his brother.

As if she had said that she didn't understand, he went on, seemingly compelled to explain. Or maybe, she thought, he was still in the process of sorting things out in his own mind. She trailed her fingers soothingly over his wrist and hand as he talked.

"All he ever wanted was to be here on the farm. He hated being cooped up. That was why he was so disruptive in school, I suppose. And it probably explains a lot of other things, as well, such as why he resented me and did everything in his power to drive me away even though he was eight years older and I was never a threat to his authority."

"He thought he might have to share the place with you someday, though, that it wouldn't be his to do with as he wanted," she speculated. Gabe had also told her how Art resented the fact that his father had willed the farm to his wife and all three of his children. He had thought, as the eldest, it should have been his alone.

Gabe nodded. "Something like that. When Dad was killed—you remember?"

She shook her head. She'd only been six, but she remembered being told years later when she'd asked why Rachel didn't have a daddy, that a tractor had rolled on him.

"Art was nineteen then, and he came right out and said that Dad's death meant the beginning of his life," Gabe went on. "I could never forgive him for saying that, but I guess now I understand it."

She looked at him, wondering if he understood because now that the farm was his alone to control, he felt that his life had finally begun. Could this have been what he wanted all along? The idea was so foreign, she couldn't accept it. Gabe had always wanted to live away from home, and not just because of his half brother's cruelties. He wanted to visit faraway places, see new sights, have adventures.

"What's made you able to understand it?"

He got to his feet and paced across the room, leaning his hands on the window frame, arms braced, staring straight ahead as if he could see out into the darkness. She saw his reflection in the black of the night outside, and ached with the need to ease his suffering. "Because I know how . . . how an obsession with something or someone can color a man's judgment. He loved this place, the land, as much as I loved the sea, and now he can't have—" Again, he broke off and stabbed a hand into his hair, turning to face her, his tortured gaze clinging to her face.

"Oh, Lord, it drives me crazy to think of him locked up the way he is! I hate *zoos* because I can't stand cages. And those are just animals. But to think of human beings . . . Why didn't they just kill him, Kathy? Why torment him like this for the rest of his life? He did a terrible thing, yes, but if he'd been a mad dog, they'd have shot him!"

"Gabe!"

"All right." His voice shook with passion. His eyes glazed over with moisture, and he blinked angrily as he swung away from her. "So now you know. I'm the kind of man who wishes his own brother was dead, the kind of—"

"Oh, love, don't!" The endearment escaped her unnoticed as Kathy swept her arms around him and pressed her cheek to his back. "Hush, now. No more. Stop talking about it. Stop thinking about it."

He turned and held her tightly, so tightly she could scarcely breathe, his face resting on the top of her head. She rubbed his back, his shoulders, whispering soothing words, offering what comfort she could. She stroked his head, his face, curled her hand around his nape and massaged gently, and never really noticed when solace was no longer what he sought from her, no longer what she offered. It was so easy, so right, to lift her face up to his, to open her mouth as his came down on it, and if some small voice inside her said "Stop," she never let it be heard.

She responded instantly, heatedly, to his beguiling kisses. Her body softened against his as if it had never forgotten how to mold itself to fit the contours of his harder shape. Her hands tangled in the thickness of his hair, her breath rasping in her throat, catching on a gasp of protest as he lifted his head.

"Oh, Lord, sweetheart," he said with a groan. "I was so damned alone when all that was happening, and I wanted you so much. I needed you."

"I'm here now," she said, blindly pulling his head back down. "And I'm not going anywhere."

"Kath . . ." It was a low, soft, growl of a sound, but if it was an objection, it wasn't a strong one, because he deepened the kiss, lifting her to the hardness of his body, moving her slowly, seductively against him. Sliding one hand up her slim waist and over her ribs, he massaged the side of her breast then cupped it. Her nipple jutted out and grazed the sensitive skin of his palm through the thin fabric of her blouse, and they both dragged in sharp breaths of pleasure.

Kathy succumbed to the thrill of Gabe's embrace, returned it, even though she knew she should have fought harder, should have pushed him away, saying, "Don't kiss me. Don't touch me. I want more than you have to offer." But the feel of his body against hers, the taste of his mouth on hers, the scent of him in her nostrils combined to create a heady rush of desire, and she parted her lips to his kisses.

He took her mouth again and again as he held her and moved under her hands as if starved for her touch. He returned the caresses she gifted him with, but gently, softly, with an infinite tenderness that made her ache deep inside, where no one else had ever made her ache.

She let her head fall back over his upper arm, reveling in the feel of the hard muscles under her neck, and opened herself more fully to him, feeling his tongue, the roughness of it, the hardness, as he probed deeply and found, with agonizing slowness, the well of sweet moisture under hers. Her hands slipped inside the cuff at the bottom of his sweatshirt and slid up over quivering muscles. She found the silk of his skin a magnet that drew her palms around his back and up to his shoulders, and she delighted in the convulsive tremors that shook his body.

"Nobody has hands as soft as yours," he murmured. "I love the way your fingers feel against my skin."

She inserted four of those fingers inside the waistband of his jeans and felt him thrust his hips against hers in response. His big fingers fumbled with the buttons on her blouse, and one of his hands slid within, fingertips brushing down inside her lacy bra, and his tremor was answered in kind.

"Oh, Gabe!" She gasped as joy surged through her. "That feels so good!"

"Kathy . . . Kathy . . ." She purred at the sound of his deep voice chanting her name, moved instinctively against his hardness, and gazed, awed, at the visible desire in his taut face as he lifted his head briefly and met her gaze, his eyes gleaming like amber under his heavy brows.

He dipped his head and nibbled at the tendons in her neck. She arched to his touch, her breathing rapid as control slipped farther and farther from her grasp.

"Gabriel . . ." It was a soft moan, half pleasure, half pain as his mouth closed over the front of her bra, hot and wet through the thin cloth, his teeth scraping over the shape of her nipple until she cried out with the need to feel him against her bare skin. He knew her so well, knew her needs, her desires, and when he unfastened the clasp between her breasts, pulling the cloth away to place his mouth against one stiffened nipple, she shuddered with delight and sighed, her knees growing weaker until all that supported her was the strength of his embrace.

"Nothing's changed in all these years," he murmured. "Still, all it takes for me to want you so bad I could howl like a wolf is to look at you. What do you do to me, Kathy? How do you control me this way?"

Picking her up, he carried her the few paces necessary and tilted her down onto the couch, covering her with the wonderful weight of his body. She moved so he could fit himself against her, between her thighs, his hardness pressing insinuatingly into her softness. He sucked a nipple into his mouth again, his hands splayed on her back, soft sounds of pleasure coming from his throat.

"I don't control you. There is no . . . control," she whispered, and arched against him as his mouth slid down her abdomen toward the waist of her jeans. "Gabe, please, Gabe, hurry! It's been so long. I need you so—"

His mouth returned to hers, cutting off the sighed words, and his fingers managed to unfasten the snap at the top of her jeans. The sound of her zipper parting to the force of his hand made her shiver with need, and when his fingers slid beneath the elastic of her panties, she wondered dimly if the high, thin intermittent sound she heard was coming from her. But no, it couldn't be. It was an insistent sound, an intrusive one, and she groaned in frustration when Gabe lifted his head, then his torso from hers.

She tried to draw him back down, because his lips were like an addictive substance and she couldn't get enough, fighting for more even when he rolled to sit beside her, his eyes burning with hunger he didn't try to disguise. "Easy, sweetheart. I don't want to stop any more than you do, but we have to."

She squeezed her eyes shut in frustration, struggling to sit up. "No!" she cried. "Dammit, Gabe, not this time! I won't let you do this to me again! If you think—"

His fingers bit into her shoulders as he gave her a quick shake. "Kathy . . . Stop it. Listen. One of the babies is crying. Oops, now both of the babies are crying." He slowly let his hand slide down her back, then around to her quivering abdomen, onto her thigh. He didn't want to leave her.

She shuddered and pulled away from him, still not fully understanding his words, only that he had, in character, called a halt to their lovemaking. She couldn't look at him. Carefully, with unsteady fingers, she refastened her bra and buttoned her blouse.

"Where did we put the babies?" he asked from the doorway.

What was he talking about? Babies?

Oh! *Babies!*

Jolted into action by a louder, stronger cry followed by a thin wail, Kathy moved briskly. "In your mother's room. I guess Angelica's hungry. She must have awakened Heidi. I'd better see to them before they wake everyone else up."

"We'll see to them," he said decisively, leading the way down the hall.

Five

"You're glad the babies cried, aren't you?" he asked, looking at the top of her head, which was about all he could see of her in the dim light of the single lamp that shone in the living room.

The question startled her, because it was as if he had stepped right into her mind. Looking up from the baby she was feeding, she met his somber stare fleetingly, and then dropped her gaze.

She sighed and quietly admitted the truth. "Yes. Yes, I am glad." When she had thought Gabe was calling a halt because of some moral hang-up of his, she had been hurt and angry, but she knew, now that hot passion was no longer hammering her senses, that it would have been wrong for them to have made love under the circumstances. If and when she and Gabriel made love again, it would not start out as a hormonal response. Not just because their bodies remembered one special night. There would have to be some kind of commitment this time. They would both have to want it on more than just one level.

"How did you know?"

"You haven't been able to look me in the eye since we came back here. You look embarrassed and . . . relieved."

She looked him in the eye. "I'm sorry. I know I probably started it. Are you glad we stopped?"

He smiled. "Not . . . entirely."

She had to laugh, and the soft sound broke the tension. "Not at all, I think. It's not because I don't want you. But there are still too many things unresolved between us. We shouldn't have been giving in to purely physical urges."

He didn't deny that those urges had been purely physical. "Things?"

She shrugged.

"Like hurt feelings?"

"Maybe. But that's a bit of an understatement, Gabe. You hurt more than my feelings."

He was quiet for several minutes. "You were the one who left, Kathy."

"Singapore, yes. But you didn't make any attempt to get me to stay."

"I know."

"And you were the one who left—originally."

"It . . . wasn't easy, doing what I did."

"That didn't stop you."

"No. It didn't stop me. And I'd do it again." He lifted a hand briefly to stem the words she might have spoken. "Oh, not all of it. To start with, I'd have kept my youthful lust in better check. Or I'd have aimed it at someone older, more able to deal with it and with me and what I wanted out of life."

She lifted her brows. "Could you have done that?" It hurt to think that he believed he could have. For her, loving Gabe had been as inevitable as the grass growing. She'd thought he'd felt that way about her too. But, she reminded herself, on his part it hadn't

been loving. On his part it had been "youthful lust."
She nearly gagged at the term.

"We're talking about having perfect hindsight," he
reminded her. "If I had known how badly I was
going to hurt you, yes, I'd have stayed ten miles
from you."

She shifted little Angelica in her arms, seeking a
more comfortable position, and tucked one foot up
under her. "I was young," she reminded him. "Resil-
ient. I survived."

"Yes. I noticed." His tone made her head snap up.
He was looking at her with what she could only
interpret as resentment and remembering, she knew,
that one night in Singapore he'd learned she wasn't
a virgin. He'd said that he hadn't expected her to be,
not at the age of twenty-seven, but she'd sensed his
disappointment, his hidden anger.

Her eyes widened. "Didn't you want me to survive?"

His sigh ruffled the hair of the baby he was feeding, and his mouth had a wry twist as he said, "I
didn't realize it until just now, until you said that
you had, but maybe I didn't want you to, at least not
so well. I . . . oh, hell, this is going to make me
sound pretty damned selfish, Kathy, but I think
somewhere in the back of my mind was the idea
that you would wait for me."

"You told me not to."

"I know that."

"Aren't you being pretty unfair?" She had a few
resentments of her own eating away at her. It was
time to air them.

"Yes," he said. "Dammit, I said it was going to
make me sound selfish as hell, but all that time, I
guess, I believed I could have it all. The adventure I
craved, the life I wanted—and you in the end."

"I see. And when was 'the end' supposed to come?"

"I never put a time frame around it, never consciously said to myself that in two years, or three, or six, I'll go back and get Kathy. But when I'd done my first hitch in the Navy and had to decide whether to sign up for another, you were in college." His gaze fixed on her. "I went to see you, Kath. You were away that weekend, skiing with friends. I only had that weekend, so I couldn't stick around waiting to talk to you. I told myself it was for the best and signed up for another hitch."

She was silent for some time, assessing the degree of pain his words brought. It wasn't something she was incapable of handling, after all. She breathed through it, slowly, evenly, until it waned and she could speak again. "And if I'd been there?"

"I don't know. Truthfully, I have to say that I'm not sure now why I went to see you. I had no set plan of action. It wasn't as though I was there to ask you to—I was just there to see you, to talk to you again. Find out how you were doing."

"For the record," she said tautly, "I was doing fine."

"I know." His voice was gentle.

"And also for the record, I'm still doing fine."

"Yes. You don't need me, Kathy. I'm aware of that."

"Oh, Gabe . . ." She hadn't meant it like that. And she did need him, in more ways than she cared to contemplate. It would be nice, though, to have those feelings reciprocated.

"No, it's all right. Like I said, it's only recently that I've come to realize that I wanted you to wait for me, expected it somehow. Even though—" He broke off abruptly. He knew, in his heart of hearts, that her waiting or not hadn't been his hang-up. His problem was with himself, and it would exist until the day he died. "We all learn to live with disappointments," he said. "And that's going to have to be mine."

She thought about a woman whose name she didn't even know who had left him and their child.

"You've had greater ones, I think."

"None that I can remember."

"Oh, come on, Gabe! Your marriage. Surely that was a big disappointment, if not an outright heart-break."

"I got what I wanted out of my marriage, Kath."

"Really? And what was that?"

He smiled. "Why, Ricky, of course."

"Ricky?" She stared at him, anger surprising her by leaping to the forefront of the multitude of emotions that struck her. "I have a big problem believing that!" Baby Angelica squirmed, and Kathy tilted her over her shoulder, rubbing her back, glaring at Gabriel, who simply stared back at her as if assessing the reaction his words had caused. He lifted Heidi up, too, and she burped.

"You're quite the expert, aren't you?" Talk about resentments!

"Try sitting her on your knee and holding your hand under her chin. When they're that little, you have to get their spines straight before they can burp." To her amazement—and her annoyance—it worked.

She put the nipple back in Angelica's mouth. "How old is Ricky, Gabe?"

"He's three."

Shock zinged through her and left a burning in its wake. *Three?* That meant that Gabe had met, fallen in love, and conceived a child within a couple of months of his having docked in England after that Oriental cruise. Or he'd already met his wife-to-be, probably even loved her, and had been simply dallying with her that magic, starry night when they'd made such wonderful love.

Or maybe he'd already been married.

No! She rejected those ideas at once. That was not Gabe's way. If he'd made a commitment to a woman, he wouldn't have been carrying on with others, no matter how great the temptation or how starry the night. That was why he'd never made commitments.

"You've known her—your wife—for quite a while, then."

He leveled his gaze on her. "I met Andrea shortly after you and I were . . . together that last time. And she's my ex-wife."

Suddenly, she remembered his comments about how alone he had been throughout the trouble with Art and about how hard it had been to be known as the brother of a crazed murderer. Had his wife been one of those who wondered about his sanity?

"Did she, Andrea, leave you because of Art's trouble?" she asked tautly, filled with loathing for the woman.

"No." He smiled faintly. "In a way, I guess you could say she married me—I married her—because of what my brother did. And she didn't exactly leave me. We agreed that as soon as Ricky was born, we'd end it."

"But . . . *why*?"

He grimaced. "Why not? It wasn't as though we were in love, or even liked each other all that much."

"Gabriel!" She gave an indignant snort. "I can't see anybody marrying for any other reason, and certainly not you. Especially since you were always so dead set against marriage. I thought you must have succumbed to the grandest passion of all grand passions."

He looked uncomfortable. "I know that's what you thought. I let you think that, but it wasn't fair. You're always honest, so I guess I owe you the same. That's why I'm trying to explain. But there are other reasons for marriage. Convenience, to name one, and pregnancy, to name the most obvious."

Something in her went cold. "I see. And since it seems unlikely, under the circumstances, that you were searching for someone convenient, I suppose that leaves pregnancy."

"That's right. Andrea was pregnant." He swallowed visibly. "But not with my child."

Kathy raised her brows and managed not to let her jaw gape open. Anger surged through her again. "You married someone who was pregnant with another man's baby? Pretty altruistic, Gabe."

Also pretty damned unbelievable. Did he think she was just off the boat? Or did he still think she was a dumb seventeen-year-old? "I've never known you to be a liar, but this time you're stretching credulity to the limits."

"Well?" she asked when he remained silent. "Why did you marry Andrea when she was carrying another man's baby, if love wasn't your motive?"

Gabriel sighed. "I told you I didn't love Andrea. That's the truth, Kath. I would never lie to you. Art is Ricky's biological father."

"Art? But—" She shook her head rapidly. Were things slowly beginning to make a tiny bit of sense? Since Gabe seemed to be having such difficulty telling the story straight, maybe the right questions would elicit the right answers.

"When did all of this take place?" she asked slowly, frowning. "The murders, I mean. And the trial. Your marriage."

"Nearly four years ago. Like I said, just after I saw you again."

She looked at him, the question burning in her heart almost written across her face. *If it hadn't happened, would we have lost these past four years?* He read her perfectly, he knew, but how could he reply? He didn't know himself. He might, had he not received that devastating phone call from his mother, given in to his immense need to follow up on his meeting with Kathy. But the call had come, and now neither of them would ever know.

"So you met Andrea when you came home to be with your mother?"

"Yes."

"And just like that you married her."

"Not just like that. I had to do a lot of thinking, a lot of considering, but in the end, there really wasn't much choice. For either of us. We had a quiet wedding in a judge's chambers, then had just as quiet a divorce soon after Ricky's birth.

"I've told you the truth about Ricky's parentage, but very few others know. A lot may suspect; I can't help that, and I don't care about them, but I wanted you to know. Legally, he's mine because I was married to his mother at the time of his birth. And he's mine in every other way that counts too," said Gabe quickly before she could go on. "I love him."

She had to smile at his vehemence. "I've never doubted that."

"But I did not love Andrea. I married her because I wanted Ricky to have the benefit of knowing his mother was married, and I wanted him to carry the Fowler name, as is his right. I know that's old-fashioned, but it was important to me. Andrea was pregnant when Art was arrested, and though she told him, he refused to marry her. I'm not all that certain it would have been allowed, anyway, and if it had been, on humanitarian grounds or something like that, there'd have been so damn much publicity that it would have been worse that way for Ricky in the end."

"Of course." She rocked the now sleeping baby in her arms, looking down at the tiny face, fantasizing for just a moment. Then, lifting her gaze, she said softly, "I'm sorry I called you a liar, and I'm glad Ricky has a dad like you."

Gabe felt a great weight lift from his back as he smiled at her. "When I knew Andrea was pregnant with my nephew and didn't want him, I wanted so badly to keep him that I was willing to do anything to make it possible. So I talked Andrea into marrying me because, well, it seemed the best solution for everyone concerned."

"Yes. Of course it was." She stroked her finger over the baby's head, amazed at the softness of the pale hair. What did Ricky look like? When was she going to meet him? Holding that other baby in his arms, did Gabe remember Ricky's infancy and think it would be nice to be a father again, or was his unofficial adoption of his brother's child his way of achieving fatherhood without the bother of marriage? "Will you ever tell Ricky?"

"I . . . don't know. Maybe, when he's old enough to understand. Of course, he'll want to know why his mother and I divorced so soon."

She couldn't help wondering what would have happened if his good sense hadn't prevailed before he joined the Navy, and if she had gotten pregnant by him. Would he have given up the life he wanted and married her? Oh, heavens, she knew he would have. And would the divorce have come just as soon after the birth of their baby?

"Does Andrea see Ricky very often?"

"No. She doesn't see him, period. When she left here, she said she wouldn't be back. She granted me sole custody from day one."

Kathy was astounded. "Why? How could she do that?"

He shrugged. "Maybe . . . seeing him, thinking of what might have been was more than she could bear. Maybe that's why she didn't want him. She said that for a time she even considered abortion, but something held her back. I'm not certain she would have wanted a baby under any circumstances, but maybe that's unfair. It could be that she simply couldn't face having one without Art." He shook his head. "According to Mom, he and Andrea really had something going; she was good for him. She was, Mom said, able to reach something in him that no one else had ever discovered. With her he was more gentle, and she adored adores—him."

Kathy found it hard to imagine the cold, remote Art commanding such depths of feelings from any woman, but maybe, as Gabe's mother said, caring for Andrea had changed Art in some way. Though obviously not in any truly important way, since he had gone so bad in the end.

"She doesn't live here now?"

"No. She's gone to live near the hospital. She visits him every week, faithfully. Lord, Kathy, she's so damned young! Nearly twenty years younger than Art, and this has destroyed her life too. I wish she'd stop caring for him, but she says she can't. Just another reason," he added bitterly, "for wishing for the death penalty."

He stared into the distance. "You know, sometimes I think it might have been fairer to Ricky if I'd let Andrea put him up for adoption so he'd never have to hear about all this and suffer because of it. So that he'd never have to wonder about whether he's inherited some of the same quirks, the way I do."

"Gabe . . ." She had to swallow hard before she could go on. "You don't honestly worry about that, do you? About yourself?"

His smile was crooked and not at all humorous. "I

have, on occasion. During long, dark nights when I can't sleep."

He laughed; a short, bitter bark of sound. "Must be one of those nights. I've never told anyone else any of this." Then he added, a nostalgic note mixed with hostility in his tone, "Like before, huh? Telling you not only my dreams but my nightmares."

Only there was one, of course, that he'd never told her, that he couldn't have shared with anyone no matter how he might have wanted to. And now, of course, it was much too late.

"Oh, Gabe, I told you mine, too, remember? But forget that particular nightmare, okay? You are so steady, so sane, so very well adjusted that you'd be crazy to think you might be crazy."

He looked at her quizzically. "Somehow, strange as it may seem, I find your words less than comforting."

"Well, you know what I mean. Everyone who matters knows you're solid through and through. There is no germ of insanity in you!"

"Thanks for the vote of confidence," he said more lightly. "So much for the nightmares. Want to hear the dreams?"

She nodded. Even knowing that his dreams didn't likely include her, she wanted to hear them.

"When Ricky's a little older, I'd like to get a manager for this place and take off. Or maybe sell it and invest the money to provide for Mom's and Rachel's shares of the property—Art's, too, I suppose—and leave something for Ricky's future. That is if Mom would agree. In the past couple of years, she's been thinking more seriously about going to live near Rachel. This whole thing with Art and—" He broke off, looking startled, and shook his head as if to clear it.

"Art and what?" she asked, but he went on quickly,

leaving her wondering what more there was that he wasn't telling her.

"She's only stayed because she thinks I need her help with Ricky—which I did at first. But things are easier now that he's in preschool three days a week. Maybe I should just buy a boat for the two of us and sail away."

"Sail away? Sail away where?" Just when she had decided to come back to the valley and had discovered that he was living there, he was suddenly taken by the idea of moving on? Of course, she thought bitterly. Once before he had seen her as a threat to his independence, and he'd had to run. It was history repeating itself.

He closed his eyes and leaned his head back, a faint smile on his lips. "Where? Would it matter? The South Pacific maybe. Island-hopping. Maybe running charters."

"You'd be a long way from your mother and Rachel and—other friends."

"I've never had any trouble making friends wherever I went. And you could join us now and then and do an article on the hobos of the Pacific." He grinned without opening his eyes. "Maybe Ricky and I and our boat would appear on the cover of *National Geographic* along with your very well known byline."

"Thanks," she said dryly, "but I believe hobos of the Pacific have been largely overdone."

He opened his eyes and looked at her. "There! See what I mean? You just finished telling me that you think I'm solid and sane and normal, yet when I offer you an incredible chance like that, to visit two handsome bachelors aboard their sailboat in the South Pacific, you back off just as quick as you can."

His tone, she thought, might have been light and joking, but she was jolted by the shaft of pain she saw in his eyes. He really did worry about how oth-ers perceived him in the light of what his brother had done. She wanted to reach out to him, to tell him again that she believed in him completely, but the moment was gone too soon, and he smiled as if to tell her that he hadn't meant anything he'd said.

Probably not even the invitation.

"I'm not going to dignify that with a response," she said tartly after a moment, then added on a more serious note, "Do you think that's why Andrea didn't want Ricky or to stay married to you? Do you believe she was afraid of genetic quirks?"

"I don't know. I didn't especially want to stay mar-ried to her, either, you know. We never shared much. Not even a room." He looked down. "Though I used to sit with her and rub her back when it ached at night."

"Does Ricky know who his mother is?"

"He knows he has a mother and that her name is Andrea, but it doesn't mean anything to him. At least, not yet. It'll be different when he's old enough to notice that most kids have moms living at home. Then he might resent her for staying away, or re-sent me for letting her go away.

"And there's another reason for the two of us to get out of here and make a life for ourselves else-where. If he doesn't go to school with kids from normal families, there won't be such a sense of loss. I can teach him. There are all sorts of correspon-dence courses that cover all the grades, and there are many kids with wandering parents who take them along for the ride. It would be good for him. He'd probably end up with a better education—at least a much broader one—than most."

"You'll convince yourself yet," she said dryly.

He looked at her and smiled crookedly again. "You think it's a lousy idea, don't you?"

She shrugged. "It's none of my business, though, is it, Gabe?"

"I didn't say that, and you didn't answer my question. Do you think it's a lousy idea?" His eyes demanded a reply, and the taut line of his mouth said that her opinion mattered to him in some way. She pretended the baby needed her attention, and the next time she looked up, Gabe had slumped sideways on the couch, still holding Heidi. Both were sound asleep.

Kathy got up quietly, put Angelica in her wicker basket, and slipped Heidi out of Gabe's gentle hold. After tucking the older baby into the cradle she had found in the basement, she tiptoed back to the dimly lit living room, lifted Gabe's feet and legs onto the sofa, then covered him with a quilt. Unable to help herself, she bent and brushed a kiss across his cheek, smelling the good, masculine scent of him, feeling the prickle of stubble, the strength of his jaw muscles. His mouth curved in a smile, and his head turned toward her, as if he were seeking the feel of her lips on his skin again.

She turned out the light. Then, with a blanket wrapped around herself, she pulled two chairs close together, curled her body into one, and put her feet up on the other.

It might not have been the most comfortable bed in the house, but it beat sharing one with two squirmy children, and kept her close to hear the gentle sound of Gabe's breathing. As tired as she was, she couldn't help wondering what that had all been about, that "hobo in the South Pacific" stuff. There seemed to be only one conclusion. Now that she was home, he was about to run again. Run scared. So why had he told her? What in the world did he want from her, that she beg him to stay? She had begged him once before when he'd been determined to leave. She was damned if she'd do it again.

This time, if the man wanted her, he wouldn't run.

And this time, if he ran, she would somehow learn to stop wanting him.

She fell asleep on the thought.

When she awoke, she was the one on the sofa, and Gabe was nowhere to be seen, but the smell of coffee came strongly from the kitchen. It was still totally dark, and there was silence all around.

Silence?

Conspicuous by its absence was the sound of the rain.

Quickly, Kathy got up and slipped into the bathroom. With that many kids in the house, she knew from yesterday's experience, use of the bathroom was something she'd better grab while the grabbing was good.

Gabe lifted his head alertly as she emerged, and shoved whatever he'd been reading under his clipboard on the table. His eyes showed he'd missed hours of sleep, and there were deep grooves drawn between his nose and mouth. Nevertheless, his smile was full and welcoming.

The sight of him warmed her right down to her toes, and something fluttered within her. She knew he was remembering, as she was, that interlude before the babies woke up. She shivered deep inside. Last night she had told him she was glad they had been forced to stop. Now, looking at him, remembering the storm of desire that he had created within her, she was no longer sure. Even if he had no intention of forming a long-term commitment, maybe she should take what was available and count herself lucky to have that much. Her heart came to a full stop as he stepped close and reached around her to hook down a coffee mug from a shelf over her head. His arm brushed her shoulder as he leaned over her and set it down, the warmth of his body close against her back. Hands free, he put both of them on her shoulders and turned her. Bending, he brushed his mouth over hers, and she sighed, softening against him, tilting her head back. These were not the actions of a man who was intent on running away from a woman, were they?

"Good morning," he said huskily.

"Good morning." Rising up an inch or two, she returned his kiss.

"Why didn't you lie down on the couch beside me?"

"There wasn't room," she said.

His arms tightened around her. "I'd have held you. I wouldn't have let you fall off."

The thought of being held in Gabe's arms all night again was thrilling, but she shook her head. "You needed to rest properly."

His smile sent delicious sensations through her. "You're right there, for sure. With you that close, I wouldn't have gotten much rest. But you know, there used to be room on that couch for both of us. Remember?"

She shivered. She remembered. "Maybe we've grown some since then."

He shook his head. "No. Not in any aggregate way. What I might have gained, you've lost."

"It's fashionable to be thin."

He let out a long breath that fanned the short hair by her temple, and let her go.

"What are you doing dressed like that?" she chided as she filled her cup. He was wearing his flying suit again.

"How would you like me to be dressed?" he asked with amused interest.

"It's stopped raining," she said crisply, sitting across from him and sipping the hot brew from her cup. "You aren't going out on patrol again, are you? The water will start to go down now."

"It might," he conceded. "But I wouldn't bet on it. It may have stopped raining here, but it's almost a sure bet it's still pouring up there." He waved a hand in the direction of the mountains Kathy knew lay virtually all around. "And as long the rain falls on that snowpack, the rivers aren't going to be able to handle it. Ours isn't the only valley flooded, you know. There was so much snow in the mountains last winter that we should have anticipated what would happen this spring."

"I thought farmers always anticipated things like flood and drought, and read the weather better than meteorologists."

"Yup," he said with a quick grin, sliding his clipboard aside and showing her the pamphlet he'd been looking at when she walked in. "That's why there's a *Farmer's Almanac*. My mother sets great store by it, and she's been a farmer longer than I have. So, I thought I'd consult the next best thing, a book on horoscopes, and see what's in store for the next week or so."

"My dad always asked old Joseph August," said Kathy, taking the little book from his hand and flipping through it at random, pausing here and there. "He said if an Indian didn't know how to read the weather, then no one did."

"Maybe Joe just knew how to read the almanac," suggested Gabe, bending down to tug on his boots.

"What's the date?" asked Kathy without lifting her head from the page.

"May eleventh. Why?"

"I think you should stay home. This doesn't sound good," she told him.

"What doesn't?"

"Mars has a vast influence over you today, and there's a malevolence in the air. Don't try to get any important projects off the ground. Grave danger lurks for the unwary," she said. "And that's just for today. Want to hear tomorrow's?"

He grinned. "Not particularly."

"Well, gee, Gabe, at least listen to the general forecast for the month." Without waiting for him to agree, she said with deadpan seriousness, "Your sun is at odds with Pluto, and Mars is in conflict with your birth sign from the ninth to the thirtieth. You're going to have a difficult month to get through. Madame suggests you live quietly, make no permanent decisions, and take no risks at all."

He laughed. "So much for Aquarius. Now yours."

She'd scanned her own. "Oh, it's nothing special. Just the usual hogwash."

"Right," he said, getting to his feet and draining his coffee cup. "It's all coming back. If you like what your horoscope reads, you believe it. If you don't, it's hogwash. Now what does it say?"

She closed the book and sat on it, laughing. "I told you, nothing important."

It took Gabe no time to lift her out of her chair and hold her with one arm as he flipped to the right page. "Ahh . . . here we are, Gemini. For today: Hmm, this looks interesting. 'Open yourself to suggestions. You have an intuitive understanding of personal concerns.' Have you, Kathy? What is your intuition telling you today?"

To get out of here before I get hurt again, she wanted to say, but he continued reading aloud. " 'The earlier part of your month will be filled with confusion and emotional turmoil, but you will overcome these difficulties. Finances may take a beating if you decide to change jobs. However, as the sun changes signs on the twenty-first, your position, both emotionally and in regards to employment, will improve. Be prepared to travel and take on new assignments.' "

He dropped the book to the table and encircled her face with his hands, then bent down and brushed her lips quickly with his before saying, "See? I told you it wasn't in your stars to live in this valley again."

"Nor yours," she murmured. "Hobo."

He shook his head. "When I said that last night, about sailing away, that was middle-of-the-night talk, Kath. Dreams only. There's no substance to stuff like that, no more than there is to what's written about the future in horoscope columns."

"You still don't believe in dreams coming true, do you?" she asked, her voice taut.

He hesitated for another moment or two as the "wop, wop, wop," of an approaching helicopter began to beat through the air. Gently, he released her and looked into her eyes for a few more seconds. "I want to. Believe that. In the middle of the night, I want it very badly. But in the daytime, I face reality."

"Yes," she said quietly. "I remember. To quote a very old friend of mine, 'Things seen by starlight don't look the same under the light of the sun.' "

"You say that as if you don't believe it."

"I don't believe it, Gabe. I didn't believe it when I was seventeen and you used it as an excuse to leave me, and I don't believe it now. I believe that people with stars in their eyes can still realize their dreams, even under a blazing sun."

"Stars in their eyes," he said. "Or rocks in their heads." He reached out and pulled her into his arms again, straining her to him, her forehead pressed into the crook of his neck. She held him tightly, feeling his muscles quiver under the palms of her hands. "Oh, Kathy," he said, his voice shaking with the force of his emotion. "It seems that you suffer from the first. And I'm suddenly afflicted with the second."

He laughed harshly, caught a handful of hair at the back of her head, and tugged gently so he could look into her eyes. "What am I saying, 'suddenly?' Where you're concerned, I've had that problem since the day they took the braces off your teeth and bought you a bra."

"Gabe?" She gazed at him, her eyes full of questions, her heart hammering hard.

"I . . . want to keep you here," he said, his voice dropping almost to a whisper. "If I could have you here, maybe I could face staying."

"Gabe—"

He cut her off, placing two fingers over her lips. "No. Don't say it. Don't say anything. Sweetheart, there are things you don't know. Things I have to tell you. But there's no time now. I kept you here when I didn't have to, because I couldn't bear to let you go. So you see, I still let some dreams carry over from the night into the day. But it was wrong of me to do that, Kath. I didn't have the right."

"Everybody has the right to his dreams," she said, her lips moving softly against his fingertips. He took them away, sliding them to the soft underside of her chin, stroking her skin as if the feel of it was something he couldn't get enough of. "Even you, Gabe." Her lips trembled and her eyes grew damp. "Even me. I want my dreams to come true, and I'm prepared to make sure they do."

He sucked in a harsh breath and shook his head. "Oh, Kath, I . . ." His voice cracked, but he went on. "I want your dreams to come true, too, love." He dipped his head, kissed her one more time, and then let her go, slipping out the door Hans swung open so he could carry in two buckets of milk.

Kathy stood listening as throughout the house the sounds of sleepy, confused children filled the air. With difficulty, she recovered her senses. She needed all of them about her, she knew, because the day had really begun. But she felt a thrill of excitement as she anticipated its end.

Six

The day ended without Gabe's coming home on the
helicopter. Kevin, the pilot, took the Mennonite children away in two loads, happily assuring everyone
that their families and farms were safe, that although the fields had sustained some damage, the
houses were untouched. When he returned after taking the second load of children home, he shut the
helicopter off and disembarked.

"I'll milk those cows for Gabe," he said. "No telling
when he'll be back."

"Back?"

"Yeah. He's gone up the other end of the valley to
Janet's. You know, where Ricky's been staying. He
wanted to spend a bit of time with the little guy.
Didn't he tell you?"

"No, but he's not answerable to me. Say, could I
hitch a ride out of here, or is the water low enough
that I can walk home? I tried it the first day and got
nothing but wet."

"You did? Why'd you want to do a thing like that?
I'd have been happy to fly you out that morning
before we started work, but Gabe said you were beat

and needed to rest before you met your dad. I understand your old man's the editor of the local rag. I
kinda wondered why you weren't in more of a hurry
to see him."

"I was in a hurry to see him. But . . ." She bit her
lip. "I thought the chopper could be better used in
rescue work than ferrying me home." Her anger rode
high while she tidied up, waiting for Kevin, but it
was mixed with an all too liberal dose of disappointment that Gabe had not been in a hurry to come
home after all the things he had said earlier that
morning. It was like having her kite carried high on
a gust of warm wind and then feeling it die, feeling
the kite of her emotions plummet to earth where a
crash of gigantic proportions and devastating effect
was imminent. All she could do to counteract it was
concentrate on the knowledge that soon she'd be
with her father again for the first time since last
Christmas, when they'd spent a month together in
Tahiti.

"Of course, it's a good thing you did hang around
up here," said Kevin, returning to the house after
milking the cows, "what with those kids needing a
place to stay and someone to look after 'em." He
poured the milk into the big glass jars Kathy had
washed earlier. "Their folks really appreciate it, you
know."

"Sure," she said, putting the milk into the refrigerator. "Glad I could help."

She lifted her camera bag and slung it over her
shoulder. "Well, I'm ready," she said, and headed
across the wet grass through the steamy, late afternoon sunshine, toward the helicopter.

"You sure you don't want to wait for Gabe? I think
he's kind of expecting you to be here and—"

"Thanks," said Kathy with a smile. "I'm sure."

From the air it was possible to see the extent of

the flooding. The water had receded a long way, and dark stains marked the walls of many buildings, some nearly up to the eaves. Other buildings had been washed away, she could see, along with chunks of roads and more bridges than just the one whose end she had witnessed, although the main one across the river in the center of town was intact. A vast wash of tangled driftwood had been left lying in the wake of the flood. And even yet, the river was three to four times its normal width in many places, with trees and parts of houses and barns sticking up like little islands.

Kevin had a car parked near where he landed the helicopter and after that, it took a very short time for him to drive her to Mike's house. She murmured her thanks, closed the car door quietly, and stood by Mike's van, out of sight of the door or the windows for a few moments, collecting herself. Overhead, the sky had darkened, and stars were beginning to shine.

Stars in their eyes. Or rocks in their heads. And then he had kissed her. She had the first one, and he had the other, he'd said, and he'd said it like a man who felt helpless—hopelessly outweighed by the odds against him. Dammit, she didn't want him to feel like that about her. She didn't want to be a threat.

But she was. That was why he hadn't come home. He'd known there would be stars in the sky and stars in her eyes, and that was keeping him away.

Shaking her head, Kathy adjusted the strap of her camera case and stepped out from behind the van. She mounted the steps to the back door, gave one quick knock, and then swung it open.

Mike, seated at the table before a plate of something she couldn't identify, turned his head to look over his shoulder. His eyes, behind his horn-rimmed glasses, were filled with surprise and light and laugher and love. He closed his mouth, pushed his glasses higher, got to his feet, and took a step toward her.

"Kath? Kathy Christiana M'Gonigle, what in the hell are you doing here? Don't you know we're just getting over a flood?"

Kathy laughed as she launched herself across the room and into his arms. He picked her up and spun her around, his boisterous laugh booming. "Here, now, what's this?" he said, setting her onto her feet and pulling a big red handkerchief with white polka dots out of his hip pocket and wiping her wet face energetically. "I told you, kid, we're just getting over one flood. We sure's hell don't need another!"

"Hi, Mike," she said, sniffing and laughing as her tears continued to flow. Then, almost in a wail, burying her face against his chest, "Oh, Daddy, I need to be home with you!" She'd planned to play it cool, lead up to things, feel him out, but now she just opened her mouth and let the words tumble forth, "I've come home to stay. Give me a job, please! Let me live here again!"

"A job?" He thrust her away and looked at her hard, alarm in his face. "A *job*?"

"Please! You always said if I wanted one I could have it. Well, I do, and I'm here, and . . . Okay, Daddy? Please?"

He stared at her, shaking his head in consternation. "Honey," he said. "I would have. I'd have hired you in a flash. You know that. But . . . Kathy . . . Babe, I can't offer you a job."

"Why not?"

He let out a long, slow breath. "Because I don't own the paper anymore."

"What?" Kathy groped behind herself for a chair, her gaze never leaving her father's face. "What do you mean you don't own the paper? What happened to it? To you? What's going on?"

"I sold it, babe. I . . . I never thought you'd want to come home, Kath. Honestly, it never once occurred to me that you might want that. Is it because . . . And how did you know he—" He broke off. "I'm sorry, honey. Truly I am. But why in the world do you want a job here?" Worry creased his face. "Are you going through a bad time? Not selling? If it's just money—"

"Oh, Daddy, of course I'm doing fine. It's not money. I don't really *need* a job here." She had to stop him from looking so stricken. "Hey, come on. Sit down and let's talk about this." She took his hand and pulled him back to the table, and he sat across from her, still looking stunned. "Go ahead and finish your dinner," she said, but he shook his head, turning to set his plate on the counter behind him.

"I'm not hungry. Suppose you tell me what you're doing back here. Seems to me that for the past—what? ten? twelve—years, I'm the one who's had to go to you if we wanted to keep the family together."

She shrugged. "I've been back a few times."

"Sure, a day or two here, a weekend there, if you happened to be flying out through Vancouver."

"You always said you liked getting away for a few weeks every six months or so, and that it gave Moose a chance to run the paper on his own."

She bit her lip, thinking about her father's huge, placid assistant with his perfectly lyrical pen. That man, who looked as if a sledge and an anvil would make him complete, could describe a daisy in terms that brought tears to the eyes. "Poor Moose. What happens to him now that you've sold the paper?"

"Moose is working for the new owners. So am I, for the time being. Just till they get the hang of things. They take over in less than six weeks. With Moose's help, they'll do fine. They're both good writers, and young, full of life. Sort of like your mom and I were when we started out." In her face, he read the sense of loss she was feeling. "I'm sorry, honey. I should have told you a long time ago. It's just that telling you would have made it more . . . real, somehow, and maybe I was trying to pretend to myself that everything was still okay."

"And it's not okay, is it, Daddy?" Fixing him with her gaze, she said, "It's not just the loss of the paper that's bothering you. Selling out . . . That's the result of some other problem, isn't it?"

He looked down at the table and outlined his placemat with the blunt tip of one finger. Kathy waited with ill-concealed impatience, then said, "Will you talk to me for heaven's sake? I told you you didn't look good last Christmas, but I let you put me off with some vague statement about needing more sun. But it wasn't just winter blues, was it? The sun didn't perk you up. You haven't sounded right for months, and your letters haven't read right." She drew in a tremulous breath, fighting terror. "Are you sick?"

His head jerked up, denial in his eyes. "I'm not sick, Kath. I promise you. I'm strong and healthy and have more good years left in me than I deserve, considering the way I've lived."

She fixed him with a sharp gaze. "Okay, so you're not sick. But there's something wrong with your life." He looked stubborn, his mouth firmly closed, his eyes narrowed in a don't-push-me glare, but Kathy was not about to be put off again. If she had to push, then she would.

"Who cares about you more than I do, Dad? Who has more right to know what's hurting you? Why did you sell the paper?"

He sighed and gave her a small smile. "All right." He got up and went to a cupboard where he took down two short, wide glasses, dumped ice into one, and left the other empty. From another cupboard he took a bottle of rye whiskey, splashed some into the empty glass, and a smaller amount into the other. He held out the icy one to her, and jerked his head toward the living room.

Kathy got up and went with him, curling into a big wing chair that she was almost lost in. He sat down opposite her and took a healthy slug of the neat rye in his glass.

She stared as the level dropped.

She reached out and took his big, hard hand in hers, offering mute support. "That bad, huh?"

"That bad. I'm fifty-seven years old," he began. "And for more years than I care to count, I've been trying to get the woman I love to marry me. Finally, she agreed." He dropped his eyes, lifted his glass, and drank again, nearly draining it. "And then, a few years back, I went and did something so bad to her that she can't forgive me. But stupidly, I kept hoping, kept telling myself that she'd forgive me, get over it, change her mind." He shook his gray head.

"She won't forgive you?"

Staring into the liquid, he said, "Maybe it's more a case of 'can't deal with things' than 'won't forgive.' She tried. I know she did. For a while she even pretended, but it was there, the gradual erosion of what we'd once had, until we had nothing in the end. So five months ago I put the paper up for sale."

She heard the heartbreak in his tone. Putting the paper up for sale had not been something he had done lightly. The pressure must have been enormous. If only, Kathy thought, she had paid closer attention, realized something was seriously wrong with her father before this. "I don't see the connection, Dad. Was it something you wrote in the paper that upset your lady?"

"There's no connection. I just want to leave here

so I don't have to see her and not . . . have her."

"Oh, Dad. Your paper," she said mournfully. "You loved it so much!"

"Yes, but what good is a life here without Gracie? I hate knowing I hurt her." He looked up at his daughter. "But I had to do it, Kathy. There was absolutely no choice."

"What did you have to do?"

"I had to turn in her son. He was a murderer. He was a vicious, dangerous man, and he couldn't be allowed to go free. I didn't know for certain that he was the one, but I had seen him there at the right—or the wrong—time, and I had to tell the police. They found his prints and—"

"Art?" she interrupted in a shocked tone. "Art Fowler? Oh, Dad! You were seeing Grace?"

"That's a polite way of putting it, hon. Grace and I had been . . . seeing . . . each other off and on since a couple of years after Matt was killed. Of course you kids never knew."

Kathy's breath escaped in a rush. Darn right they'd never known! At least she hadn't. She frowned. Had Rachel? No. Rachel would have told her. Had Gabe? Had that had anything to do with his rejection of her?

Thoughts caromed in her head until she managed to bring them under some control.

"But . . . did you think we'd object to your getting married?"

"It wasn't that. Neither one of us wanted to be married then. We were very fond of each other, liked each other's company, and, well, we needed each other. We were together whenever we could be without risking any gossip. We both had kids to think of, kids we didn't want doing what we were doing, and if you had known what we were doing, how could we have told you it was wrong? The age-old parental dilemma."

"Because what's right for adults isn't necessarily what's right for kids," Kathy suggested lamely, still reeling with shock that she and Rachel had never suspected what was going on between Grace Fowler and Mike M'Gonigle.

"I don't understand why you didn't want to get married then. Wouldn't it have been best?"

Mike grinned. "And put you and Gabriel into the same house?" He shook his head. "We couldn't take that risk. You'd been making calf-eyes at the boy since you were twelve years old."

"Dad, that's not true! I didn't really notice Gabe as anything more than Rachel's big brother until I was fifteen."

He shook his head. "You were noticing him, all right, though you may have been too young to realize you were, or to realize just how heady that kind of noticin' can be to a young guy. No, we didn't want you two in the same house. Also, there was Art. That worried me, if it didn't seem to worry Grace. In truth, though, I never discussed Art with her or my feelings about him. Not until after."

He swirled the remains of his drink, watching the small eddy he created in the bottom of his glass. Kathy watched it too. The rye was exactly the same shade as Gabriel's eyes.

"Not until it was too late," Mike went on musingly. He frowned and shook his head as if answering some inner question, drained the last of his rye, and got up to pour some more. Kathy put her hand over her glass which was still half-full.

"It wasn't something I could ever tell Grace," he continued when he'd sat back down, "but I didn't trust that boy. Never did, never could. There was always something underhanded about him, something disturbing. Maybe we could have rode herd on you and Gabe, honey, but I sure didn't want you having to put up with Art's sneaky, mean ways."

"But later? I mean, we all did grow up. We left home. Except for Art, and Grace could have come here to live. There'd have been room for the two of you."

"I know. And that's what I finally persuaded her to do. I thought that once Gabe had gone to join the Navy and you were away at college, we might do it then, but she said we'd been going along fine the way we were so long, we may as well wait until Rachel was settled somewhere. I think, in the back of her mind, Grace knew, too, that Art was not to be trusted. She wouldn't come live here and leave Rachel up there with her brother, and this place would have been pretty cramped for three adults. Then, when Rachel got engaged to Graham and planned to move down to the coast, it all seemed to be going to work out fine and—how the hell did you know about Art, anyway? I very carefully didn't tell you."

She answered his question with one of her own, one she felt she had a right to have answered.

"Why not, Dad?"

He took another swig and set his glass down, rolling its bottom edge around in circles on the arm of his chair, leaving little damp marks where there had been hundreds of such damp marks over the years.

"Because I didn't know if you'd ever really gotten over loving Gabe. And because just before all this happened, his mother said he'd seen you recently on his cruise ship, and she thought things might be starting up all over again between the two of you. Then, with things working out the way . . . they did, I didn't want you hurt."

He looked up, his face a mask of pain. "And I have

to admit I was afraid that maybe you'd condemn me, too, as Grace did, and Rachel."

Kathy got up and held her father close. "Never, Daddy. How could I condemn you for doing what you had to do, for doing what was right? I'd have done the same thing."

"Even if it meant sending your lover's brother to prison for the rest of his life?"

"Yes," she said, "and with far less compunction than you for doing what was necessary. Honorable men," she went on angrily, "how they suffer from being that way. And make others suffer along with them."

"Meaning what? That I shouldn't be making Grace suffer? I know that. I wish I could turn back the clock. But it's done and—"

"I didn't mean that."

"But you've suffered because of some man's honor."

She nodded. "You referred to Gabe as my 'lover.' He wasn't, Daddy, not before he joined the Navy."

"Good. So my vigilance paid off."

"Your vigilance had nothing to do with it. It was him. He always refused my offers. That was the honor I meant."

"And the suffering."

She nodded. "He wanted—wants—his freedom more."

"Kathy, honey, I have to tell you this. Gabe is here, in the valley. Up there." Mike gestured toward the hill behind the house. "That freedom you think he wants, well, he's given it up now. He has a little boy, but no woman. He—"

"I know all that, Dad. I've spent the past couple of days marooned up there. How do you think I know about Art? I—"

She broke off at the sound of pounding on the

back door, and Mike got to his feet just as the door opened.

"Mike, I have to talk to you. I have Kathy up at my place. She's been there since the day before yesterday. She thinks she's come home to stay, but she doesn't know about your selling the paper. She's—"

"She's here," said Kathy, getting to her feet and stepping around her father.

"Kath!" Gabe lifted a hand to reach for her, then let it drop. The expression on her face did not encourage such a gesture. Her green eyes glittered with either pain or anger, or both. Her face was pale, her mouth tight, and her fists were clenched at her sides.

"I . . . thought you'd stay up at the house tonight. I told Kevin to—"

"Leave me there? Odd, but Kevin recognized me as an adult able to make her own decisions. I decided not to stay up there but to come home. Sorry to disappoint you."

"But we needed—need—to talk."

"I thought we'd done plenty of that last night. And the night before. To say nothing of this morning. And of course, our talking only left me more confused than I was before. That's all talking with you ever does to me, Gabe, so I don't see the point in doing it."

"We didn't talk about anything important, Kathy. Not the way we have to. We just touched issues."

"I think we touched them enough. Besides, why should I have stayed? Kevin didn't know when or if you'd be back."

"I had to drive up to the other end of the valley and spend some time with Ricky, explain to him why I couldn't take him home with me tonight."

"I see. And why couldn't you?"

"Kathy . . ." Gabe swallowed hard. "Do you mean

why, or do you mean what did I tell him? I told him his school was still too wet, that he'd be better off staying there and going to preschool with Luke, Janet's son. But the reason is that I wanted some time to . . ." He let that trail off, and Kathy finished it for him.

"Clear your decks?" she asked, then added in a deadly, quiet tone, "Or was it more along the line of battening down your hatches?"

"Kathy," he began helplessly, but this time, it was Mike who interrupted.

"If you two will excuse me, I have to go and see a man about a . . . wet basement," he said, grabbing his jacket off a hook by the door and shaking it to make sure the keys to his van rattled in the pocket. "Maybe several men, several basements. I won't be back soon. There must be at least half a dozen of them around this town."

The door banged behind him, and Kathy turned to walk back to her chair. Gabe lowered himself slowly into the one Mike had been sitting in. Elbows on his splayed knees, he linked his hands together, bouncing them slightly up and down. His eyes, she saw, were tortured.

"I had every intention of going home. Home to you," he added softly. "To talk seriously, to sort things out once and for all, and maybe to make love with you."

Her insides curled with pleasure at the thought of making love with Gabe, but she forced the sensation away from her consciousness. "Did you? Nice to be let in on your plans, Gabe. A little late, but nice."

"Kathy, this morning you must have known what I was saying to you. I couldn't keep quiet about it another minute, though I know I should have waited for this evening. What happened? Did you have second thoughts?"

"In a way I guess that's true, though I didn't real-ize it until you failed to come home. This morning you were saying exactly what you used to say, Gabe. That you wanted me, but that you didn't want to want me. When you didn't show up this afternoon, what else was I to think other than that you'd decided to be 'sensible' again? That was the term you used to use so frequently." She shrugged and let out a long breath. "What you call being sensible, I call Gabe Fowler running away. I hate thinking that you want to run from me as much as you're drawn to me. I'd never know where things stood between us, Gabe."

He came out of his chair and stood before her, holding out his hands. "Come home with me, Kath," he said huskily. "I'll show you how 'sensible' you make me feel. I'll show you exactly how things stand between us. I'll show you that I'm not running."

Slowly, she shook her head. "No, Gabe."

"Dammit, you know you want me!" He ran a hand through his thick hair leaving it sticking up all over, and Kathy had to fight the urge to smooth it down.

"Yes, I do," she said.

He blew a frustrated breath toward his eyebrows. "Well? What are we waiting for then?" When she neither moved nor answered, he hunkered before her, his eyes pleading. "Kath, don't do this to me. Okay, so maybe I screwed up this afternoon, but I was trying to balance your needs and mine and my son's. It isn't easy, because I want to do what's right for all of us."

He got to his feet again and paced away from her. "Dammit," he said, spinning around and facing her from across the room, "Dammit, all right, so I was wrong to put Ricky first. But he's just a little boy, and I thought you were adult enough to understand and—"

"Gabe!" Kathy shot to her feet and strode to him,

grasping his upper arms and shaking him . . . trying to shake him. It was like trying to move a stone pillar. "Knock it off! I don't care that you put Ricky first as you say. I think it's right that you went and spent time with him, made sure he was happy and asleep before you left. Dammit, what kind of opinion do you have of me if you think I'd think otherwise?

"What makes me furious is that Kevin would have been more than willing to take me out in the chopper that very first morning, and you knew it. Yet you decided that I would stay at your place, for whatever reasons you had in the back of your mind."

He shook his head. "Those reasons didn't stay in the *back* of my mind very damn long at all," he said. "Within minutes of our landing that first night, I knew why I'd brought you home with me. Because you're mine, Kathy. Because you belong with me." His fingers slid into her hair, cradling her head as he tilted her face up and kissed her slowly, running his tongue along the half-parted seam of her lips.

She shuddered with need but managed to turn aside before she could be persuaded to give in to it. "No, Gabe. Stop it." She put her hand on his chin, holding his head away. "Sit down again. You're the one who said we need to talk."

"I need this more," he said, crowding her fingers aside and nuzzling her neck. "Dammit, I can't talk. I can't think. All I can do is respond to this . . . this power . . . that you have over me, a power to disrupt my life just when I thought it was going to be steady and secure and boring as hell. Just when I thought I could learn to like it that way!"

His kisses were quick and hot and wet, brushing over her face, landing wherever they happened to land as she turned her head from side to side, turned it slower and slower, until he captured her lips in a long, deep, and drugging kiss.

He lifted his head moments later, and said roughly, "I was doing fine until I was winched down on that cable and found you sitting on your car like a small, drowned Buddha, smiling through your terror, not showing one hint of surprise at seeing me there."

Her lips trembled, wet and tender from his kisses. "I was surprised, all right." She slipped out of his arms and went back to her chair. She needed the support for her wobbly legs. His kisses had always been able to do that to her. Just as they'd always been able to make her want more and more.

"Not half as surprised as I was," he said, coming to crouch before her again, his hands on the arms of her chair, effectively imprisoning her. "Nor half as glad."

"Gabe, that's not true. Mine was the life in danger, after all. I was more glad to see you than I had been to see anybody ever before."

"But not because it was me. You'd have been glad to see old Mr. Peters from the post office if he'd been on that cable."

She wanted to laugh at the thought of the short, fat man from the post office attempting rescue work, but she'd heard the unconscious plea in Gabe's tone and responded to it. "Yes," she said, touching his smooth, freshly shaved jaw. "Because it was you. Oh, Gabe, don't you know anything about me?"

"I must have forgotten. Teach me," he said, and her laugh was caught by his mouth as he swept her out of the chair and sat down in it, holding her on his lap. Reaching up, he turned off the lamp, darkening the room so that the only light came through the archway from the kitchen. He slid a big hand into her hair and gently tilted her head back, nuzzling his mouth against her neck in a manner that made her toes curl up inside her socks. Her breath left her lungs in a sobbing rush, and she nearly forgot to draw it back in again.

"I can't teach you anything," she said weakly. "You know it all."

"Come home with me, sweetheart," Gabe whispered against the lobe of her left ear, then nibbled at it. "We have to start getting things sorted out between us."

She pushed him away and held him off with one hand, feeling the heat of his breath across her face, seeing the hunger in his eyes as he looked at her. "The way to sort things out properly is to . . . talk," she said unsteadily, not really meaning it.

"I think I've forgotten how to talk," Gabe said, taking her hand and removing it from his throat, placing it around the back of his neck where she felt the softness of his hair under her palm. Her fingers curled and slid higher, deeper into his hair.

"Well, try anyway. And let me go."

He didn't let her go, but he did start talking. "Last night you told me that there were still too many things unresolved between us," he said. "And I do want to resolve them, but each time I look at you, get close to you, all I want to do is join our bodies together again. I can't think straight. I'm not trying to rush you, but you need to know how it is with me. I want to take you home to my house. I want you in my bed, warm and willing and wanting me as much as I want you."

Kathy acquiesced as she felt his tongue slide between her lips, just the tip of it, stroking the soft, moist inner sides, teasing her until she gasped with desire for more and opened to him.

She heard him groan, felt his body stiffening under her, and nestled closer when he parted his thighs to settle her between them. His arms were a wonderful prison from which she never wanted to escape, and she enfolded him in her own, straining to get closer, closer.

When they broke apart, Kathy ached with arousal and need. Her heart hammered hard, her breath came in quick, short gasps, and she could only look at him, wishing she knew what was going to happen to them, wondering if she would be able to withstand the agony of losing him again when it happened. Because it would. One day, the need to be gone, the pressure of his dreams, would become stronger than his need for her, and he would go. At the moment he thought those dreams were unattainable, but when he came to realize that they were within his reach, he would leave her. But for now . . . oh, Lord, for now, was it wrong to want this, to accept this?

"Kathy . . . ?"

"What?" She could scarcely force the word out. She placed both hands on his throat, not necessarily to hold him away.

"I think we should cool it a bit. Until we go home." His voice was as warm as honey and vibrated like a fine organ against her palms. She squeezed her eyes shut and turned her face against his chest as his hands came up and covered hers, trapping them between his neck and his palms, holding her very still as the passion died down. Even when she was more or less calm again, Kathy felt herself trembling.

"You're the one who started it this time." Her fingers curled around his throat, and he took his hands from hers, leaving them free, nodding his agreement. He had been the one to start it. He was also the one to call a halt. As usual.

"Are you planning on strangling me?" he asked, and she shook her head, sliding her hands around to the back of his neck.

"You're planning something. I can tell. Or thinking of something I might not like. What is it?"

"If you think you might not like it, why ask?"

"Because I need to know what's going on inside you. There have been too many times I've let you get away without telling you what I feel, without learning what you feel. Without knowing what you want."

"You know what I want."

His eyes glittered. "Do I?"

"I think you do. You said you wanted me to be willing." She drew in an unsteady breath and slipped off his lap, standing before him. "I'm . . . willing." Slowly, she unbuttoned her blouse. With unhurried grace, she slid the sleeves off her shoulders, down her arms, letting the garment fall. Then, reaching behind her, she unhooked her bra. Her hands were trembling, but she forced them to cooperate as she lowered the cups down her breasts until her jutting nipples caught the light and cast a shadow of her silhouette against the wall.

"Kathy . . ." His breath hissed in and then out. "Not here. Not in your father's house."

She popped the snap on the waist of her jeans. The sound of her zipper was loud and incredibly erotic, and her voice was soft as she said, "Yes, here, Gabe. Now. You may have started it, but this time I mean to see that you finish it."

Seven

He got to his feet as if he couldn't help himself and stood watching her. She shimmied out of her jeans and stepped free of them, nude now but for the briefest of panties.

"I'm showing you willing," she said. "Are you going to help me or not?"

He swung her up into his arms, his mouth on hers, the fabric of his shirt abrading her nipples to even greater hardness. He mounted the stairs, rushed up and thrust open the door to her room, then laid her on the narrow bed of her girlhood, in a room he'd never entered before, but which had lived in his fantasies for so very long.

Kathy felt the cold bedding under her, then Gabe's warmth and weight pressing her down, and with a surge of passion, she clung to him. Somehow, loving him there, being with him like this in this forbidden place, amplified her responses, made her act provocative and wildly wanton. She slid her legs apart, one clinging to his thighs, the other hanging off the bed, her arms twined around his neck as she kissed him the way she had in all her dreams.

Lifting his head, he gasped and stared at her, then tore himself free, standing and tugging his shirt off over his head, not bothering with buttons. His jeans clunked to the floor with the weight of his belt and wallet. Up on one elbow, she watched him, aching with need, and then he joined her on the bed again, clasping her in his arms, rolling her onto the warmth of his now-naked body, his eyes closed, his face filled with bliss as he felt her skin against his.

"You're cold," he murmured, running his hard, callused hands from her shoulders to her buttocks. How could that be? she wondered dimly. How could he think she was cold when she was burning with a fever like never before, but then it didn't matter because he was whispering, "I'll warm you. Kiss me the way you did before. Please. Oh, Kath, I need you so damn much!" He didn't wait for her to comply, but cupped her face between his hands and took her mouth in a deep, thrilling kiss. His powerful legs locked around her so that when he rolled her under him, there was no break in the contact of their skin, and she was no longer aware of any sensation of cold against her back. She was aware only of Gabe, of his touch, his scent, the feel of his moist, hot breath on her.

His lips moved over her face, down her throat, to her shoulders and then her breasts. His tongue moistened a nipple, causing it to peak into a hard point, the sensitive skin around it puckering as he slowly drew it into his mouth. His soft suckling created an ache in her womb, and she cried out. Arching toward him, she held his head in her hands as he began to pull harder on her, increasing the heat that flooded her body, making her writhe under him, begging silently for more. His mouth moved to her other breast, tugging at her nipple until she nearly fainted with pleasure. She clutched his shoulders, feeling the rippling muscles under her palms, then smoothed her hands down over his back, reveling in the texture of his skin, the hardness of his flesh, the strength of him. Each breath she dragged in was laden with the scent of him—warm, musky, sexy. Sliding a hand down between their two bodies, she reached for him, aching to give the same kind of pleasure she was getting.

He jerked back convulsively. "No!" he gasped.

"What?" She blinked up at him, her mouth atremble, her entire being aflame. "Why?"

He stroked his lips over hers. "Don't look at me like that. Just don't touch me—yet."

"Gabe . . ." she protested, half-laughing. "What's the matter? Can't you take as good as you give?" Once more, she slid her hand down his lean waist, across his abdomen, her fingers stroking softly, tangling in his tight curls. He shuddered, thrust himself into her caress, groaned, and then moved away from her.

"Please, don't rush things," he murmured, then carefully slid her panties off her. His hands on her thighs were gentle, pressing against their inner sides as he whispered, "Put your legs apart, love. Let me touch you." She trembled all over when he began stroking her again, testing the wet silk of her desire, parting her warm flesh more erotically with each stroke, sliding two rigid fingers right inside her. She arched upward against his hand, her knees rising instinctively, falling apart as her head lolled loosely against the mattress, and her eyes fluttered shut.

"Stop!" she cried, her breath catching in her throat. " I don't want . . . I . . ."

He stopped what he was doing and rolled her onto her side, drawing her back against his chest, her buttocks against the urgent hardness of him, and ran his hands down her front.

She placed her own on them, holding them to her swollen breasts, tilting her head forward as he rained erotic little kisses on the nape of her neck, her shoulders, her arms, down her spine. When one of his palms spread over her abdomen, her muscles contracted, quivering under his seeking touch. She moved sensuously against his body and felt his response leaping, thrusting against her. He held her firmly when she would have turned in his arms, murmuring, "No, love. Please. Ah, Kath, I want to make this so good for you."

"You are. It is. But I want you in—"

"Soon." As his hand slipped lower, fingers combing through the tight mass of curls at the juncture of her thighs again, one finger found and stroked her throbbing center. She stiffened again in mute protest, then went soft when he crooned to her, "Relax, my darling. Let me love you." He rubbed gently in that manner, again and again, sliding only that one finger along the moist groove between her thighs until she moaned and began to move in a rhythm that rotated her buttocks against him. He made a sound somewhere between pleasure and pain, and quickly turned her onto her back again, kissing her breasts, while his hand continued the stroking below.

Kathy thought she was going mad. "Gabe. Please, Gabe," she begged. "I want . . . I want . . . Gabriel . . . Oh, Lord, don't. No more. No more. I can't—"

"You can, darling." He slid his hands and mouth over her breasts and stomach, down her legs, then all the way back up.

She could only gasp and surge against him again and open her mouth for him as he kissed her, his tongue plunging deep inside with that rapid in and out motion that drove her wild with need. Her arms tightly around him, she pressed herself to him, her body rocking into a stronger rhythm that he met and copied with his plunging tongue in her mouth.

When he broke the kiss to place his mouth where his hand had been, she was beyond control and convulsed when his tongue touched that sensitive nub. And then it was there upon her, that rushing, quaking sensation, unique and associated only with Gabe, and it sent her over the edge to that place she had been only once before, and only in his arms. With a sob, she felt the memories rush over her along with the climactic shudders her body was experiencing, and without knowing she was doing it, she wept. Gabe drew her tightly against his chest, holding her until both storms had passed.

"I won't leave you this time," Gabe said raggedly, and Kathy realized she had been begging him not to, just as she had before. "I promise, love, don't worry. This is now, Kathy. I'm not going anywhere."

She believed him. At last, she could believe him, but she couldn't speak, couldn't tell him. She could only cling to him and relive the moments of her total surrender to his mastery, again and again. Nestled in his arms, she never wanted to stir, never wanted to think again. Just to be was enough.

"Are you okay?" he asked several moments later. Without looking at him, she nodded, tucking her face down against his neck, content to breathe in the scent of this man of hers.

"Honey?"

"I'm fine."

"Then look at me." She resisted the tugging of his hand, and he laughed in delight. "Are you shy?"

Reluctantly, she let him turn her face up. "I guess so. I'm not as experienced as you might think."

"I don't think about that," he said gruffly. "I just

think about how good I can make it for you and how
quick I can make you forget any—" He broke off and
punched the pillow. "Hell! I wasn't going to say anything about that, you know. I lied to you. I do think
about it. I've thought about little else since Singapore." His voice was hushed as he added, "I try not
to wonder if you're . . . comparing."

"Oh, Gabe . . ." She was more touched than he
could begin to know by this evidence that he wasn't
as sure of himself as he pretended. "You do such
fantastic things to me. You always could. I've never
forgotten. And I don't make comparisons." She
smiled, tracing the shape of his mouth with one
finger. "But if I did, you know you'd be the leader
every time."

He touched her lips gently with his, moved his
hands over her body slowly, lovingly. "Such heat,"
he said. "You make me burn. You make me tremble.
You make me happy to be alive, Kathy."

His tenderness choked her up so that she couldn't
answer except to put one hand on the back of his
head and pull him down to her, and deep within her
body the banked fires began to lick and curl and
flame again, and this time Gabe didn't let the in-
ferno grow only within her. This time, he joined her
in it, and as he entered her she flung her head back
with an exultant cry, her legs wrapped tightly around
him, lifting high as he plunged into her.

She moaned, caught up in his rhythm, looking at
his intent face with dazed eyes. "Oh, yes," she said.
"It's good like that. Gabe, oh, Gabe, don't stop!" She
tightened spasmodically and involuntarily around
him, and he increased the tempo of their joining
until they were cast adrift, but together this time,
her inner convulsions coming at the right time to
trigger his.

A long time later, he rolled onto one elbow and

drew a finger from her shoulder to the tip of her left hand. She shivered, and reached out to pull up the crumpled quilt that had somehow ended up on the floor.

"Cold?"

She nodded, suddenly, ridiculously, having to fight tears and a terrible tightness in her chest. She rolled away from him, her face to the wall, the cover and her arms wrapped around herself. After a moment, she felt his hand stroking her back from nape to tailbone through the thick blanket.

"Kath? What's wrong?"

"I . . . nothing." She clenched her teeth tightly shut to keep them from chattering as the heat of their loving began to leave her body. How could she feel so apart from him after having been so close? What was the matter with her? She felt exactly as she had that morning four years ago with the sounds of the docks of Singapore in her ears and her body aching from his loving, and Gabe, with empty eyes, walking out the door. Only now, it was her soul that was empty.

"Then turn over and look at me," he said softly, his hand on her shoulders outside the quilt, tugging at her insistently. She didn't want to, but she couldn't refuse him that much. She turned, but drew her knees up toward her chest, forming herself into a tight ball as she opened her eyes and looked at him. It was like seeing a stranger, one whose picture she had seen many times. The face was familiar, but she suddenly realized she knew nothing, really, of the personality behind that face.

Was the Gabriel she had known as a teenager the same man who now lay propped on one elbow, looking down at her, his face shadowed, his hair backlit almost red by the light in the hallway? Was he the same bearded mariner she had met again four years before? She didn't know. She didn't know him. And maybe, after all these years, she didn't even know herself or where she fit with him. If she fit with him.

"A little depressed?" When she didn't reply, only squeezed her eyes shut to block the tears, he went on. "It's not unusual, you know, after such spectacular loving. To come back to the real world after flying so high has got to be a downer. But if you'd let me hold you, we could make it better together. And if we talked, maybe we could make some sense out of our lives." She only shook her head and turned her face down into the covers.

"Don't shut me out," he said, swinging his feet to the floor, giving her some space but keeping one hand on her shoulder. "I need you so much tonight."

After a moment, she sat up beside him and lifted a tentative hand to touch his cheek. He put his arms around her, rested his face on the top of her head, as if he, too, were seeking comfort. She sighed, replaying his words in her mind. Even now he couldn't hear what he was saying, couldn't recognize the significance of his words: *I need you so much—tonight.*

Presently, she lifted her head from his chest and slid away from him toward the headboard.

He scrutinized her face for a long moment and then nodded slowly, as if sensing the depth of her inexplicable withdrawal. "I still think you should come home with me," he said, reaching for his jeans, tugging them on. She shook her head. Taking the coverlet with her, she left the bed and walked to the window, looking up toward where his house stood, across the river and beyond the poplars. It—and he—seemed in that moment as distant as the moon that shone down over the valley.

"I'm sorry," she said. "I just sort of want to be alone right now."

"Why?" he asked, his voice low and strained.

She sighed. "Because I'm feeling very strange—ambivalent about us. I'm sorry."

"Isn't what just happened what you wanted too? If it wasn't, Kath, you gave one hell of a performance." His hands on her shoulders turned her from the window.

"You know it's what I've wanted since I was sixteen years old."

"Then where does the ambivalence come in?" He gave her a small shake. "Do you even know what you want, Kathy?"

She couldn't reply. Maybe she didn't know what she wanted. Oh, she wanted him all right. But she still wasn't sure she could take the limited commitment that was all he was willing to offer. Commitment was so important to her, and unless he was ready to make one as great as hers, could she make even a temporary one to him?

Clutching the quilt, she headed down the stairs.

"Where are you going?" He followed, slinging his shirt around his shoulders.

"Just . . . downstairs."

"Just . . . away from me," he said mockingly. "Aren't you the one battening down her hatches now, Kathy?"

"Gabe, I have a lot to think about. So many new bits of information floating around in my head. My emotions are all tangled up. Our parents, for one thing. You know about them, of course?"

"Of course."

"Well, dammit, why didn't you tell me? You had plenty of opportunities over the past few days—such as when you were telling me about Art. You could have said that his crime caused trouble between my father and your mother, who, up until then, had been conducting an affair under our very noses for years and years and—"

She heard a hint of shrillness creeping into her tone, and broke off, drawing a deep, steadying breath before seating herself in her father's big chair and going on.

"Didn't you think I'd be interested in that? And how long have you known about them, anyway?"

"Only since I came back," he said evenly, "and I decided it was your dad's place to tell you about it, not mine. But what does their problem have to do with you and me? If they're in love, Kathy, it's up to them to work out their own differences."

"Did you ever blame my father for what he did? I mean, going to the police with his information."

Gabe felt as if she had punched him in the gut. Blame Mike? How could he, when Mike had had the courage to do what he himself had failed to do so long ago? Lord, no, he didn't blame Mike; he blamed himself for bringing all this trouble on everyone. He shook his head. "Not for one minute," he said emphatically. "But there were times when I wished he hadn't been a witness, that he'd never been put in the position he was in." He crouched down a foot or two from the chair where she was curled, leaned closer, cradled her head in his hands, and went on.

"Mike cried, Kath. On the stand. He broke down and cried and looked at my mother and pleaded with her not to hate him."

Kathy leaned her forehead against his chest and wept softly. "And you can say that it has nothing to do with us? If we were together, it would affect them both. It would hurt them both."

He embraced her for several minutes then let her go, wiping her face with the palms of his hands. "I know. But, Kathy, be sure of one thing: No matter who it hurts or how badly, you and I are going to be together. After all these years apart, we deserve that, don't we? Don't we deserve to be happy? For just as long as we can?"

For just as long as we can? Not "forever"? Dammit, why couldn't she be content with what Gabe wanted? Why did she have to keep yearning for "forever" from him? Her eyes flooded again, and he gave her an impatient shake. "Now, don't! Just cut it out. That's the one thing I can't stand for you to do."

He held her for a few minutes more, then he stood abruptly, facing away from her, his fists clenched.

"I think I'd better go now. You're right. Your emotions are confused, and you're in no shape for any more talk." He turned back to her, tension in his every muscle. "And neither am I. I'll see you . . . soon."

His good-night kiss was rough, filled with need and still unslaked desire, and in the few seconds it took, his body hardened against hers, nearly destroying his resolve to leave her time to think things through. But as he always had where Kathy M'Gonigle was concerned, he ignored his own physical pain and turned from her, closing the door softly behind him.

"Why didn't you go with him?"

Mike waited until the red light over the door of his darkroom went out, then he knocked and entered, the question on his lips.

Kathy turned from the rack where she was hanging strips of negatives to dry. She glanced at her father, then turned back to her work, examining each frame critically before she hung the strip.

"I've got some great shots here," she said.

Mike closed in and peered. "Looks like the end of the world."

Kathy nodded. "I thought it was. The end of mine, anyway. That was just after I crossed the bridge. I was standing by the car watching it break up when the water came up around my knees in a rush."

Mike stepped back and looked at her, his eyes narrowed. "And then what?"

"And then I shoved a few important things into my camera bag and got on top of the car. After that, Gabe came down out of the sky. Angel Gabriel. On his beam of light."

Mike did as Gabe had done. He palmed her face dry, but it didn't stay dry long.

"Why are you still here?" he asked. "Why aren't you with Gabe?"

"Because I'm not really what Gabe wants, Daddy. I'm merely what he's willing to settle for."

"Oh, babe," said Mike, "that's a harsh thing to say about the guy. And how do you know it's true?"

"I can't tell you that. I just do."

"So you came home for nothing? Did you burn any bridges?"

Kathy took another strip of film from a pan and hung it on the wire to drip. She looked at Mike over her shoulder. "I came back because I was concerned about you. I didn't know Gabe was here. When he rescued me, I thought he must be on vacation." Turning back to her work, she said, "Four years, Dad. Why didn't you tell me he was here? Why didn't you tell me any of this? Art, Grace, you know."

"I explained that. At first I was too sickened by everything, and then when Gabe married that woman, especially in light of what Grace told me about his meeting you on shipboard, I didn't want you hurt. You never told me about meeting him then, Kathy. Why?"

She shrugged and emptied a pan, rinsed it, then set it to dry near the sink. Looking at the rolls of film still remaining in their cans, she washed her hands and decided they could wait.

"I don't know. I suppose because I was trying to convince myself it was all over, that meeting him hadn't meant anything to me."

"But it had?"

"It had."

"And it still does."

"It still does." She looked at him with sad eyes.

"What are you going to do now, Kathy? I mean about where to live, where to work? This house is yours whenever you want it, babe. I never intended to sell it. All I let go was the business." He lifted his shaggy brows. "I might be able to get the paper back, you know. The couple I sold it to are reasonable folks, and I have a sneaking hunch they took it off my hands out of sympathy."

Kathy put her hands on her hips and leveled a serious look into her father's eyes. "I want to ask you a question," she said.

"So, shoot."

"I want an honest answer."

"When have I ever given you less than that?" Mike grinned. "No, don't answer that. You'd just mention all the times I didn't want to tell you there wasn't really a Santa Claus." He sobered, then added, "Go ahead. Ask away."

"Do you want the paper back."

He hesitated, his gaze on hers, then smiled ruefully with a shake of his head. "No. The truth is, I was glad to get out from under it. I did love it. For so many years it was my life. After your mother died, you and the paper were all that I had to keep me going. But then there was Gracie, and it became a hardship to have to spend so many hours running around doing things other than being with her."

Kathy hugged him tightly. "Oh, Daddy, I wish I could fix things for you!"

"Hush. No more than I wish I could fix things for you. But now we have to think seriously. What are you going to do, since I sold your birthright out from under you?"

"Go on doing freelance work. I didn't intend to quit. Just . . . curtail it somewhat so I could spend more time with you. I never worry about earning a living. I can do that anywhere. What about you?"

"I've still got my contract for that thrice-weekly column in the *Vancouver Gazette*. And now there's talk of syndication."

"That's great, but I didn't mean earning a living. That I know you can do anywhere, too, and I'm sure the sale of the paper gave you enough to retire comfortably wherever you want—except you're much too young to retire. Where do you plan to live? Vancouver? You'd hate the city, wouldn't you?"

"I sort of had my eye on a great little community called Lions Bay, up on Howe Sound. It's close enough to the city to make traveling in easy, yet far enough out to be quiet and peaceful."

"Oh, sure! Trading floods for landslides!" Kathy was familiar with that strip of shoreline. "Nice move, M'Gonigle."

As if she hadn't spoken, he continued, "However . . ." He took her hand and walked with her out of the darkroom, flicking the switch behind him and shutting the door. Back in the main part of the house, he slipped an arm over her shoulders. "Where I live, my little chickadee, depends largely on you. The older I get, the more I want to be near my only child. One of these days you're going to surprise both of us by getting married and producing a grand-child or two for me. I'd kind of like to be able to dandle them on my knee, spoil them, you know."

Kathy puffed a long breath up toward her ragged bangs. "Boy! I really blew it, didn't I? Coming back here. Here, where you most definitely don't want to be."

"But if here is where you want to be, here with Gabe, then so be it. Here is where I will stay. I can write my column just as well in my den here as I could in sight of the ocean. Maybe better. I know more people in this neck of the woods, get more good gossip."

"I'd like to be near you, too, Daddy, but I could move to Lions Bay, you know. And there's no guarantee that Gabe is going to want me to stay. In fact, I'd say the odds are against it."

He turned her to face him, his big hands on her upper arms, his eyes, as green as her own, deeply serious.

"Kathy, if you want Gabe, don't let anything stop you from having him. Don't waste any more years than you've already wasted. Go after him. If you love him, don't let him get away the way I let his mother get away."

"I don't think it's going to be that easy. Just 'going after him' won't do it. I'm greedy, Dad. I want it all. And he's never said he loves me. He's never asked me to marry him."

Mike looked at her soberly. "Maybe he's waiting for you to ask him."

She blinked, shocked by his suggestion, then her eyes flared. "He'd better not hold his breath!" She sniffed. "But we were talking about you. You're important to me as well, you know, and if my staying here would make you unhappy, then I won't do it."

Mike's smile was closer to a grimace. "Honey, I'm unhappy no matter where I am. It wasn't my happiness I was trying to achieve by leaving, but Grace's."

"If she loves you, your leaving isn't going to achieve that."

"Okay, maybe it wouldn't make her any happier, but it might bring her a measure of peace in which to do some healing. I haven't given up on her, you know. I won't, ever. And I don't want you to give up on Gabe. He needs you. And that nice little kid of his needs a mama."

Kathy felt tears flood her eyes and looked at the ceiling in order to hold them back. It didn't work, and she buried her face on her father's chest as his arms came around her. "It isn't fair, Daddy! It just isn't fair!"

"What isn't?"

"I don't want Gabe to need me that way, as a surrogate mother for his child."

"Maybe he needs you for more than that, hon. Don't sell yourself short. And don't sell Gabe short, either. If all he'd wanted was a stepmother for Ricky, he could have had his choice of a couple of dozen these past few years. Now, I think you need to get to bed." He held her back from him and studied her face, frowning.

"I didn't see a suitcase, so I guess you lost everything." She nodded. "Dammit, Kathy, you almost lost your life, too, if I'm not mistaken in what those negatives show. I'm not sure I want to see the prints."

She laughed huskily. "Neither am I, but maybe I'll feel differently tomorrow. Good night, Daddy."

He kissed her cheek. "Good night, honey."

I'll see you. Gabe's last words to her echoed in her mind. For four days and four nights she waited for him to make good on them. She didn't spend the time idly, though. Her car had to be dealt with, and her insurance claim put in. It would take weeks before all the insurance claims from the valley were processed, so in the meantime, she was making do like everyone else who had lost their belongings to the flood. It was in the aftermath of that flood that she had lost the most, she thought one night, lying in her narrow bed up under the eaves of her father's house. But could she really be said to have lost something she had never had? Gabe hadn't come to her, but neither had she gone to him. She ached for him with every breath she took. Why was he staying away? Was it to give her the breathing space she had asked for? Or was it because it was easier for him not to have to make a decision?

What if Mike had been right? Maybe it was going to be up to her to ask Gabe to marry her. She knew that man of old, knew his highly developed sense of responsibility when it came to her. Could it be that he had never asked her to marry him because he truly believed it would be bad for *her*? The thought was extremely novel, and she toyed with it, watching shafts of moonlight coming in around the edges of her shade. She lay there for a long time with her eyes open, staring at the ceiling. Finally, knowing she wouldn't sleep, she arose and slipped into her clothes before going down to the kitchen. The moon was nearly full, and it was bright enough for her to read the face of the clock on the wall. 1:08. She sighed, filled the kettle, and set it on the stove. Maybe tea would help. Maybe some of her father's whiskey in the tea would help even more.

It didn't. She sat at the table and leaned her chin on her hands, no nearer to sleep than before. 1:33.

She stood, reached for Mike's jacket on the hook by the back door, and gave it a shake to listen for the rattle of keys. Fishing into one pocket, she pulled them out and cast a glance back at his bedroom door. He snored.

Feeling like a guilty seventeen-year-old, she slipped out of the house. This time, though, her guilt was compounded by the fact that she was taking his van without permission. Never before had she stooped to theft, she thought as she closed the door softly behind her. Before, she had run on silent feet across the dewy grass to where she knew Gabe would be waiting near her back gate.

She started the van and drove out onto the road. This time, Gabe wouldn't be waiting for her. This time, he didn't know she was coming to him. She wondered if he would welcome her and trembled as she drove.

Eight

Gabe, too, lay looking out at the moonlight. He had no shade drawn, and it flooded his bedroom as he sat propped against the headboard, his knees drawn up, his arms folded over them. He could make out the clump of poplars that hid Mike M'Gonigle's house from his view, and as he had years before, he tried to picture Mike's daughter asleep in her bed. Then her hair had been long and curly, and he had envisioned it spread darkly across the white of her pillow. Now it was short and curly, crisp and soft all at the same time, and his fingers itched to feel its texture. The only picture that formed in his mind was of the two of them, not on that narrow bed of hers but in his, loving the night away.

Why had he left without her that night? And why hadn't he gone to her before this? This wasn't the way it should be. She should be here by his side. Then he'd be able to sleep, knowing he would wake up with her in his arms, and the distance that had yawned between them since the other night would be a thing of the past.

He shook his head. Tomorrow, he knew, the gulf

would be even wider, and it was all his fault. If he had convinced her to come back home with him, they'd have had most of their problems resolved by now.

"Ah, hell, who are you trying to kid?" he asked himself as he got out of bed and went to the window. "Those problems are unresolvable. You know damned well you can't keep her here. If you have her, it will be on the short term, never the long term. And is that what you really want?"

Gabe shook his head, ran his hand into his hair, and went into his son's room. Ricky slept, as he always did, as if his life depended on it, totally dedicating his entire body to the process of recharging for the next day. With a smile, he bent and covered the little boy, kissed his cheek, and left, closing the door softly behind him.

He knew, though, that he was still far from sleep, and walked down the stairs to the kitchen, where he opened the microwave oven to give himself a little light, then pulled a bottle of rum from the top shelf of the cabinet over the stove.

Medicinal rum, his mother called it. Neither of them were great drinkers, but she kept rum around in case of severe chills, firmly believing in its restorative powers. Well, tonight he was chilled, right through to the bone, but it was a spiritual chill, not a physical one. He poured an inch of rum into a glass and stood looking out the window, sipping on it. He frowned as a vehicle came lurching up the potholed driveway, headlights sweeping across the window where he stood. Mike's van. He recognized it in the moonlight, frowning, expecting the big man to emerge—with a shotgun, he wondered, a grim smile crossing his mouth. No, Mike wouldn't have his shotgun out. Not yet.

For about the ninety-ninth time in the past four

days, he was caught up in the knowledge that he had taken no precautions when he'd made love to Kathy. For the first time since he'd been scared out of his mind by a Navy training film dealing with disease, he'd forgotten his "raincoat." He bent his neck, pressing his forehead against the cool glass of the window. Lord, what would it be like, watching Kathy's body swell with his child?

His eyes widened slightly, and his stomach clenched as he saw her step out from behind the wheel, marching determinedly toward the porch.

Carefully removing all expression from his face, he swung the door open and stood back, waiting for her.

"Oh!" She stepped in. "I thought I'd have to wake you up."

"No." He stated the obvious.

"You . . . don't have any clothes on."

He shut the door. "Sorry. I forgot." Oddly enough, he had done just that.

She sniffed the air. "You're drinking."

"Yeah. I couldn't sleep. You want one?"

"I put some rye in my tea. It didn't help."

He set his glass down on the counter. "Then this probably won't do me any good, either." Drawing in a deep breath, he let it out slowly, his eyes on her face.

He watched her eyes focus on the half-packed suitcase on the end of the table, the basket of laundry not yet folded on the floor. He saw stark emotion flicker across her face as she said, "Going somewhere?"

"Yeah. I have a month-old nephew I've never seen. Ricky and I are going down there for the weekend."

"Oh."

For some reason he felt compelled to answer the questions she was very carefully not asking. "I'm coming back. I planned to call you before I left."

Then, just as compelled, he had to ask one of his own.

"Why are you here, Kathy?"

"Because . . ." She swallowed and forced herself to go on. "Because I want to be."

"There's not enough to hold someone like you."

"Yes there is. You," she said softly.

She saw his chest rise and fall as he pulled in another long breath. "I don't think so. Not for long, Kath."

"Yes. Forever, if that's what you want."

He turned and dug in the laundry basket on the floor, as calm and relaxed in his nudity as if he were completely alone. She continued to stand there, half-turned from him, her heart aching inside her chest, her stomach churning, her eyes burning, while Gabe tugged on a pair of jeans. As he walked toward her, he pushed his arms into the sleeves of a shirt. Stepping around her, leaving the shirt unbuttoned, he picked up his drink and opened the fridge.

Frustrated and angered by his silence, she said, "I'm not talking about us necessarily being together here, Gabriel. Just . . . together. Wherever you want."

"You might as well sit down," he said, pouring a generous measure of cola into his rum. He filled a glass for her and set it in front of her as he took his place on the other side of the table. "Okay, let's talk about that."

Something in her rejoiced that he was at least willing to talk, yet when he started talking, she didn't like the trend his thoughts were taking. He sipped his drink. "No matter what I might have said a few days ago, I can't just up and sell this place, even if my mother doesn't come back. As far as I'm concerned, this is her home. So, unless she wants to let it go, I don't see any options for me beyond staying and running it for her."

"You mentioned a manager."

He shook his head. "Middle-of-the-night talk, Kathy."

She glanced at the moon-silvered window across from her. "What do you think this is?"

His smile was bitter. "I'm trying to be practical now, even if it is the middle of the night."

"You were 'practical' so often before, even though it was the middle of the night, Gabe, and look where that got us. Nowhere." She hesitated, wanting to ask him something important, but she was afraid. She made herself do it. She couldn't hurt any worse than she was hurting now.

"Mike told me that you'd written to your mother about having seen me four years ago. She seemed to get the impression that you . . . had hoped that meeting might lead to others. That we might . . . get back together again. Was that what you wanted then?" *And if it was, why did you let me walk away from your ship in Singapore?*

Though the last question was silent, it hung between them like an electric sign.

He shrugged. "Mom may have read between the lines something I'd have liked to happen. At least while I was in the act of writing that letter. But I knew then that it wasn't meant to be. Just as it isn't meant to be this time."

"Isn't it? When you left my place the other night you said we were going to be together, Gabe. Yet four days went by and you never even called to say hello. You've changed your mind?"

"I said 'together for as long as possible.' But yes, I guess you might say that I've changed my mind. Over the days and nights I came to see that it wouldn't be—" *Right*, he'd been going to say. He amended it. "—enough."

"That's what you said last time. That having a girl

back home might be great for you, but it wouldn't be enough for me to be attached to a guy who was thousands of miles away.'"

"Only this time, the tables have been turned. I have to stay, and you get to go."

"It doesn't have to be that way, Gabe."

"No? I think it does. I think it will be that way." For the first time, his face showed some emotion, and his voice cracked as he said, "How can I ask you to stay?"

Her heart grew to impossible proportions inside her chest. It hurt. It hurt so bad, it made her bottom teeth ache. Funny, only Gabe could make her feel like that. But if it was so funny, she wondered why she couldn't laugh.

"Are you?" she whispered. "Are you asking me to stay with you, Gabriel?"

"No." His voice was no louder than hers. Across the table, she could see his knuckles shining white as he wrapped both hands around his glass. "I'm not—" Better she think he didn't want her than to have her know the truth, only there was no way he'd ever convince her he didn't want her.

"I don't have that right."

"What if I give you the right?"

"Please, don't do this. There is nothing here for a woman like you, Kath! You're bright and successful, with the world out there waiting for you. That's why I didn't follow up what happened on that cruise, because I knew I was wrong for you."

"Wrong for me? How?"

He wanted to tell her, yet the fear held him back. How could he tell her what he really felt? That he wasn't worthy of the love and trust she was offering him, because when it came to the crunch, he'd been so intimidated, so terrified, that he'd kept quiet when he should have talked. If it had been impossible for him before, it was even more so now. How could he say, *I let my father's murderer go free because I was afraid to tell, and because of that he killed again.* He couldn't. Kathy had integrity, something he'd lost years ago, if he'd ever had it. Could an eleven-year-old kid have honor? Maybe at that age he hadn't put a name to it, but he'd sure as hell been old enough to know right from wrong, and he'd let a wrong go unpunished. Kathy would despise him for that. She had the same kind of integrity as her father had, the kind that had forced Mike to call down the law on the head of his lover's son. If she knew what Gabe had done the first time he'd suspected Art had killed—what he had not done—she'd look at him with contempt. It was bad enough that he hated to face himself in the mirror; how could he bear to see the same kind of cold condemnation in her eyes? No. It was better this way. At least, even if he didn't have her love, he had her respect. If he told, he'd have neither.

"I asked you what's *wrong* about you . . . for me."

"I can't explain. But trust me, it's so. I had to let you go then, and I have to let you go now."

"Gabriel." She shoved her chair back from the table. "I plan to make it very, very difficult for you to do that, you know."

His laugh was without humor. "It's difficult enough, Kathy. There's nothing more you can possibly do."

Kathy got to her feet slowly. "No? I begged for your love once before, Gabriel. I don't intend to do it again. But I know you love me."

He stood watching her, his face a mask, and for several heartbeats she was sure he was going to deny it or refuse to answer. Then he said, "Yes." His voice was rough and ragged. He cleared his throat. "Yes. I love you."

His admission went straight to her head, sending it

reeling dizzily with joy. She smiled at him. "That's all I want or need to know," she whispered, and the sound of the zipper at the front of her jeans was loud in the deep silence.

"Oh, Lord," he said, half-laughing, thrusting a shaking hand through his hair. "Once you learn how to reach a guy, you don't forget, do you?"

She stepped free of her jeans and tugged her sweater off over her head. "That's just the trouble, Gabe. Where you're concerned, I've never been able to forget anything."

"You didn't put on any underwear," he said. His voice was unsteady.

"I didn't want to waste any time."

He touched one of her breasts, lifting it slightly, rubbing a thumb over the already hard tip. His hand was unsteady. "Dressing or undressing?"

She stroked her fingertips down his cheek. "Either." She swallowed hard. "Gabe. Love me."

"Yes," he said, "I will. I . . . do."

Pain stabbed into her at the bittersweet undertones in his voice, but she forced herself to hear only the words he had said. They were what was important now. Whatever else haunted him could be worked out later.

Lifting her high against his chest, again he carried her up a flight of stairs, and laid her across a bed, but this time he was placing her on the one where they both knew she had belonged all along.

"Mine," he said, smiling down at her in the glow from the moon. Then a spasm crossed his face. "Why have you kept on loving me, against all the odds?"

"I don't know," she said, pulling him down to her, loving him so much she wanted to cry with the intensity of her feelings. She wrapped herself around him, kissing his face, his ears, his neck, then his mouth. "But I have . . . and I always will . . . because you're mine, too . . . as much as I'm yours," she whispered between kisses. "I love you more than I can tell you, but I had given up hope of ever hearing you say the same. All those years . . . I never stopped. I only . . . thought I did. Oh, Gabriel, I'm sorry I thought I didn't love you. I'm sorry for—"

"No," he interrupted fiercely, clapping a hand over her mouth, knowing what she was about to apologize for, unable to bear hearing her say it. "No one matters but you and me, now. We are what count. We won't discuss that part of our pasts."

"Okay," she murmured, and he felt her lips move against his palm. He removed his hand to cover her mouth with his own, kissing her until they both soared crazily into the stratosphere.

She gasped. "Gabe!"

"I know. I know." He had no breath. Stroking her from neck to hip, staying very still until the wild passion in both of them eased to a steady, potent glow deep within, he whispered love words to her. As his breathing slowed and the rate of his heart tapered off, he sighed, and began the whole sequence again, only at a seductive, unhurried pace, stroking her body, watching the darkness of his hand on her moon-creamy skin, all his senses heightened to a new awareness.

"Do you plan to torture me like this for long?" she asked silkily, nibbling at his shoulder through the fabric of his shirt. "Because if you do, I promise equal measures of the same for you."

"Really? What kind of tortures do you have in mind?"

"First, I'm going to get these clothes off you." Up on her knees, she straddled him, tugging at his shirt, sliding its front panels apart, nuzzling his chest.

He rolled and shed the garment, coming back to lie there, smiling up at her. "And then?"

She attacked the snap of his jeans. Mischievously, he tightened his abdomen, making it impossible for her to manipulate the snap. Grinning, she grasped the tab at the top of his zipper and tugged it down over the hard bulge there. Sliding her hand inside, moving it slowly, sensuously against the hard ridge of his sex, she said, "You forgot your underwear too."

He popped his snap and lifted up, shucking his jeans in one easy sweep of his hands. "I didn't forget." His voice was breathless. "You said you had . . . other things in mind. Such as what?"

She told him, and his eyes widened, glittering.

"I look forward to that. I've looked forward to it for years, but I can't let you do it now, or it'll be all over before it begins." He flipped her easily onto her back and performed a few more elements of torture on her until she was gasping and whimpering, then he eased up, soothed her with his kisses, rubbed gently with his hands, his breath fanning her neck.

She touched the puckered scar under his eye, running one fingertip around the shape of his ear, feeling the heat rise higher and higher inside her, but willing to play his game and make it last. It would be worth every moment he made her wait, she knew, and even the waiting was a sweet, pleasurable kind of agony. But if she thought for an instant that the moments of waiting were going to be less agonizing for him, then he was wrong. Provocatively, she slid one thigh between his and moved it fractionally, back and forth, up and down. He growled a low warning, and her laughter gurgled out.

He froze, lifting his head to look at her. "I love to hear your laugh. I used to lie awake nights and try to remember exactly what it sounded like, all husky and warm and sexy. Do you have any idea how many nights of sleep you've cost me over the years?"

She shifted slightly and tilted her head back as he kissed her throat. She purred and smiled when he lifted his head to look down at her again.

"You are so beautiful, Kathy."

"You make me feel beautiful," she acknowledged. Against her she felt his body tighten, felt the muscles flex, felt his rigid manhood pulse spasmodically. He shifted to the side when she moved again to touch him, then captured both her hands in one of his and pinned them over her head while he bent over her, kissing the undersides of her breasts, avoiding her nipples even when she tried to get them to his mouth. "Tease," she accused, laughing, then gasped when he lost the battle.

"You love this kind of teasing, don't you?"

"Don't talk with your mouth full," she whispered, but he was right. She did love that kind of teasing, when he was the one doing it. "Why are you doing this to me?" she asked moments later, her voice thin and high.

"Because you respond so well."

He let her hands go and sat up, gazing at her damp, heaving breasts. "I love the way you react to my touch."

"Good," she said, "because now it's your turn to react."

She rolled him to his back, capturing his powerfully aroused flesh and moving her hand in a steady, strong rhythm while attacking one of his pebble-hard nipples with lips and tongue and teeth. "You'll kill me!" he complained on a sharply indrawn breath. "Ahh . . . Kathy . . . Stop."

Smiling, feeling triumphant, Kathy got to her knees beside him, dipping her head to run her lips down his belly, feeling it quiver. "You don't want me to touch you?"

His hands clamped onto her waist, holding her back from her intended actions. His eyes were half-shuttered, glittering between his thick, short lashes.

"I want you to touch me. But not so much. Not so fast. I want to savor, love, and I think you do too. Come here. Let me hold you. Let me kiss you. I want to feel you in my arms, close to my body. Remember how it used to be? Remember the hours we used to spend just holding each other? It was so wonderful, Kathy. Come here."

She didn't move, managing to resist the powerful pull of his hands, the even more powerful pull of his gaze. "Then, we had clothes on. Then, we—at least I—hadn't known what awaited me."

"But now that you do, don't you know how sweet it can be, anticipating?"

"Yes," she whispered, anticipating to the point almost of insanity, "but enough is enough."

"Where you're concerned, there'll never be enough for me," he said, reaching for her again, "but you still won't make me rush it."

Smiling, she cupped her hands under her breasts and lifted them, brushing her thumbs over her nipples, reddening and hardening their already pointed peaks. Bending, she offered them to him. "Won't I?"

"Don't tempt me," he said with a groan, kissing first one, then the other, drawing that one deeply into his mouth before flipping her onto her back and taking her lips in a deep and evocative kiss that threatened to get completely out of control. But control it he did, and Kathy groaned in frustration.

"Gabriel . . . dammit, if you don't let me play, too, I'll take my toys and go home!"

He levered himself off her and looked down into her eyes, instantaneous laughter mingling with the shimmer of passion. "So eager, so impatient, so untruthful."

She clung to him, loving him, laughing with him. This was the Gabe she had searched for, yearned for: Quicksilver changes, laughter to ardent desire and back again in seconds.

His laughter stopped, and his hand cupped her jaw.

"Ah, love, you're right. Enough is enough." He took her shoulders in his hands, tilted her down onto the bed, ran the tips of his fingers from her palms to her ankles, then turned from her and carefully prepared himself.

"My beautiful woman," he said. Then, as if arranging her as a sacrifice, he guided her legs apart, knelt looking at her for several seconds, and moved over her quickly, thrusting inside her waiting body.

With straining muscles, she reached to hold him, catching his rhythm at once and moving with him toward and into a glorious climax that carried them high, then let them tumble slowly back to earth.

"You are so precious to me," he murmured as the peace of total release enveloped them, and their breathing became regular. This time there was no depression, no emotional withdrawal, and Kathy curled against her lover, sleeping the first good sleep she'd enjoyed in more than a week.

She awoke to the scent of coffee and the brush of something soft over her cheek. She opened her eyes. Gabe stood over her, tickling her nose with the tail of her blouse.

"Look what I found, Ma. A nekkid woman in my bed. How do you suppose she got there?"

She tugged her blouse from his hand and tossed it a few feet away. "I like being naked in your bed," she said, wadding her pillow behind her head. "I hope you're not trying to tell me to get dressed."

"I love having you naked in my bed," he said, sitting beside her, taking the other pillow and stuffing it behind her as he held her up. Settling her back, he handed her a cup of coffee. "But I also have a little son who makes a habit of getting up about five-thirty every morning and coming in here to make sure I'm awake."

And of course, it wouldn't do for his son to find a naked woman in the bed. Kathy knew that. Her intellect accepted it. Her heart, however, rebelled. What if she were Gabe's wife? Or going to be his wife? Would he object, then, to his son's finding her in his bed?

"And what time is it now?" She set her coffee cup on the nightstand and reached for her blouse, pulling it on and buttoning it.

"Ten past five."

"You're up early."

"I have stock to see to before I go."

She was silent, staring into her coffee. Go? For a minute, she didn't remember that he was going out to the coast for the weekend, then she lifted her head, nodding.

"Of course. I'll get out of your way."

"Kathy . . . it's not like that, you know. You could . . . No. No, that wouldn't be a good idea, would it?"

"What wouldn't?"

"I was going to say you could come with us, but . . ."

But what? she wanted to ask. *But you don't want to take me because your family might get the wrong impression? Or I might?* Instead, she said, "No. It wouldn't be a good idea," and grabbed her jeans, tugging them on.

"I'll be back late Sunday afternoon. I'll see you then."

Kathy ran a hand through her short hair, straightening it—more or less—and shook her head. "I don't think that would be a good idea, either, Gabe." She glanced around. He'd brought her shirt and jeans but not her shoes.

"Hey, listen," he said, capturing her and holding her in front of him, forcing her to meet his gaze. "I meant what I said last night. I love you. That's not going to change, Kathy. I have to go down to Rachel's. It's the baby's christening this weekend, and I'm his godfather. I'm not abandoning you, sweetheart."

She fought against the tightness in her throat. She struggled to sound reasonable, to feel reasonable, but she didn't. All she felt was this entirely too unreasonable sense of hurt. "I know. But . . . I have to go home now. Let me go."

"Not like this. Not while you're angry. What's gone wrong? Where am I screwing up again?"

"Oh, Gabe, you're not!" She slid her hands up onto his chest, feeling his warmth and strength, wishing she could take some of it into herself, bolster her faltering faith with it. "It's me. I just can't deal with this . . . not knowing."

"Not knowing what? You know I love you. You know you love me. Why can't we just take things day by day, grow closer and closer, finding our answers in that intimacy. What else can be important?"

"It's important to me to know where this is going to take us. I hate not knowing if our loving each other is going to lead in the direction I want it to lead. I thought for a while I could accept that, told myself it would be all right, that I could be a fatalist, believe what will be, will be. I wanted to go along with you, love you a little more each day, and let that be our answer. It may be yours, but . . ."

"It's not yours?" he asked, his mouth a hard line of tension in his pale face.

"No. It's not."

"And what is?"

She hesitated. *Maybe he's waiting for you to ask him.* It was easy for Mike to say, wasn't it? But . . . she had never liked cowards, had she, had never wanted to be one. "My answer is what Rachel has, what your parents and mine had. Permanency. Belonging. For all time." She drew in a ragged breath.

"Gabe, will you marry me?"

His breath puffed out sharply. "God!" he said. "You don't make things easy, do you?"

Dropping her hands from his chest, she stepped away from him. "I told you I wasn't going to," she said, and walked out of his bedroom, closing the door softly behind her.

Gabe stood staring at the panels of wood, his heart hammering high in his throat. Distantly, he heard the rough sound of the van's engine as Kathy started it.

With a groan, he sank to the side of his bed and buried his face in his hands, not lifting his head until Ricky said, "What the matter, Daddy? You got a upset tummy?"

Nine

When Mike came down the stairs, looking a little ragged around the edges, Kathy guessed he'd heard her go out and had stayed awake until she returned.

"I'm sorry," she said. "I disturbed you, didn't I?"

He shook his head, but it was true. She'd disturbed him, all right, though not by going out. He'd heard her and had smiled, knowing that what she was doing was right. It was her coming home when she had, and the pain he'd known she was suffering as he lay there listening to her weep quietly.

He'd wanted to go to her but knew she wouldn't want him to, not just now. Whatever personal demons she was fighting she would have to fight alone. With a great strength of will, he'd stayed where he was, thinking of the nightmares he had soothed, the little-girl heartaches he had eased, the disappointments he had helped her face. All those tears, all those wounds, and he was the one she had come to in her grief. Why, he wondered, was it so easy for a father to wipe a bloody knee, kiss it better, and stick on a bandage? All the years of doing that had made him believe he would always be able to take care of things for Kathy, and to know now, when his child was really hurting, that parental love and caring simply weren't enough was hard. There were things a bandage wouldn't fix, hurts a father's kiss couldn't ease. A mother, he knew, could have gone to her, could have helped at a time like this, but Kathy had no mother. All she had was him. He'd gotten half-out of bed then, but stopped. Nope, good ol' fixer-upper Dad was stymied.

Now, seeing that she wanted to pretend everything was all right, he gave her a mock-serious scowl and said, "You and I have something to discuss, young lady."

Kathy's eyes widened. "What's that?"

"Theft. Auto," he said. "Good for at least five years, I'd say."

"Oh, please, Judge, give me a break. It was a first offense, and I'll never do it again!"

He pondered, rubbing his chin with one hand. "Well, what if I release you to your father's custody for the next couple of days or weeks or years—or however long it takes?"

"Only," she said after a few moments, "if my father agrees to lock me in my room at night to keep me home and safe."

"Know something, honey? There ain't no such thing as safe."

She nodded. "Yeah. I think I spent the last hour or so discovering that. I took your advice. I asked Gabe to marry me." She drew little circles on the tablecloth with the handle of her spoon. Then, lifting her gaze to Mike's, she said, "He didn't say yes."

"Did he say no?"

Kathy let a small, mirthless laugh escape. "Now that you mention it, he didn't."

"Well, then?"

She smiled and got to her feet, giving her father a

brief hug of thanks. "I'm going for a walk. See you later." As she walked, she wondered if she was crazy to take such comfort in the knowledge that Gabe hadn't said an outright no.

If he did come back on Sunday, Gabe didn't get in touch with Kathy. She had, she knew, only herself to blame; she had told him not to. Yet each time the phone rang, she lunged for it, but it was never him. Monday passed, Tuesday, and when the phone rang again just after lunch on Wednesday, Kathy went on with the article she was roughing out, knowing the call would be for her father.

"For you, hon," said Mike, and she felt her head go light, but it was not Gabriel. A soft-voiced man identified himself as the father of Hans, Giesela, and Marta. His community, he told her, was having a dinner to thank the people who had helped them so much during the flood, and they would be honored if she would attend.

She thanked him, accepted, and hung up, biting her lip, torn between adolescent excitement that she'd of course be seeing Gabe there, and resentment that he'd taken her at her word and not come to her. What if she didn't show up? He'd be expecting to see her there, wouldn't he? If she didn't go, then maybe he'd come looking for her.

"Damn!" she muttered. "I won't let him do this to me!"

"What's that?" asked Mike absently.

"Nothing," she said. "Just talking to myself."

"Something wrong?"

"I've been invited to the Mennonite community for a thank-you feast on Thursday evening."

"This is a problem?" asked Mike. "Some of the best cooks in the world live there."

"Yes, I've heard, but what does one wear to a dinner with Mennonites?"

"Something opaque, longer than a mini, and not too revealing around the neck and shoulders, I'd imagine," Mike said.

"Oh, that's good. The red track suit I picked up the other day should fill the bill," she said dryly.

"Kathy Christiana M'Gonigle, don't you dare! You'll wear a dress if I have to buy you one myself."

"With thick black stockings and a little white cap?" she asked cheekily, and then sobered. "Seriously, Dad, I don't know what to wear."

"You don't have to do the dark stocking and white cap routine, that's for sure, so don't look so worried. The cap is something individual women choose or don't choose to wear, depending on the strictness of their upbringing, I suppose. And not all of the families out there are all that strict. They're nothing like the Amish. They're quite progressive, use machinery for their work, and have a telephone in their village." He eyed her narrowly. "And I suppose, also, that Gabe will be there, and that, not the dress, is what's really bothering you."

Kathy shrugged. "I suppose," she said, but she did take great care in choosing a new dress for the dinner party.

Following directions, she drove the fifteen miles of back roads to the isolated valley that held the Mennonite community. She parked near the lighted hall which was rapidly filling with people, heads bobbing in greeting to the guests, such as she, who approached somewhat more slowly.

She caught up with Kevin, the helicopter pilot, his girlfriend, who he introduced as Janine, and

Jim, the copilot. "I remember you," Jim said. "You're the woman from the roof of the car."

Kathy had to laugh. "What a way to be remembered. I understand I have your sharp eyes to thank for my life." She added seriously, "And I am grateful, Jim. Thank you more than I can say."

"Nah," said Jim dismissively. "One of the others would've spotted you if I hadn't. And where's ol' Gabe? Didn't he bring you?"

"I have my own transportation," she said pleasantly, and then Kevin was introducing her to several members of their host community. She was duly thanked by the parents of all the children she had cared for, was given little Heidi to hold for a few minutes, and then Giesela caught her hand, taking her away to show her some of the more exciting desserts the women had prepared.

She was talking and laughing with a group of teenagers when she felt a touch on her arm and went very still inside. Slowly, she turned. The laughing young people moved on, leaving the two of them in a small pool of silence.

She wanted so badly to break that silence, but there were no words she could think of to say. She could only look at him, wondering what he was thinking, wondering if this moment was as awkward for him as it was for her. She had asked him to marry her. He hadn't said yes, which, in spite of what her father said, was tantamount to having said no. If the tables had been turned, would she have been able to walk up to him as casually as he had approached her?

She searched his eyes. No. His approach had not been casual, it had only looked so for the benefit of anyone who might have been watching. There was a tension about him, an intensity in his gaze, and she knew that for him, this moment was as difficult as it was for her. She knew, too, that no matter what either of them might be thinking or feeling, now was not the time to talk about it.

Gently, she smiled.

Gabe smiled back and a measure of peace filled her soul. "Hi, Kath." His voice sounded rusty as if he hadn't used it for a long time.

She swallowed hard. "Hi."

"I called this afternoon to offer you a ride out here tonight, but there was no one home. I stopped by on my way here, and Mike said you'd already left."

"Yes."

"I wanted to bring you."

"I didn't know."

"I see you've been shopping." He held just the tips of her fingers, and lifted her arms out from her sides, letting the dolman sleeves of her blue dress fall in graceful folds toward the narrow silver mesh belt around her waist.

"You look beautiful."

"Thank you." She glanced around at what the other female guests were wearing. Her knee-length dress did not look out of place.

"You look nice too." His gray, three-piece suit was superbly cut and fit his body exactly right. His hair was freshly trimmed and he smelled heavenly. She lowered her eyes before he—or anyone else—could see that she was ready to devour him.

"Uh, how is Rachel? And the new baby?"

"Just fine."

There was no message for her from Rachel? Not even a secondhand hello? If there was one, Gabe didn't pass it on. "Who does the baby look like?"

He shrugged. "I don't really know. A little like Ricky, I think."

"That doesn't help me much. I've never met Ricky."

"No," he said, as if she had asked to meet his son and he was refusing permission.

She was saved having to search for conversation after that very definite conversation stopper, because the announcement came that dinner was ready.

The speeches were mercifully short, if the grace was long and involved, and the food was wonderful as well as overly abundant, and Kathy felt obliged to sample a bite or two of everything she was offered. By the time the desserts she and Giesela had admired were brought out, she was sure she'd never be able to force down another morsel, but she managed one or two morsels, and two cups of the most delicious coffee she had ever drunk.

It was late by Mennonite farm standards when the gathering began to break up, and Kathy walked out to her car with Kevin, Janine, and Gabe.

"Does that thing run?" Gabe asked, referring to the little gray car she had bought to get around in while waiting for her insurance claim to come through.

"It got me here, didn't it?"

"I'm more concerned about it getting you home," he said. "Get in and start it. I'll follow to make sure you make it all right, so wait for me at the entrance to the road." He loped away to the other side of the parking lot.

Her car started more quickly than it had at the beginning of the evening, and ran respectably all the way home. Pulling in beside Mike's van, she got out and waved to Gabe, who had tucked the nose of his pickup in behind. "There," she said, when he opened his door and came to where she stood. "See? I told you it ran."

"And every time you change gears, little puffs of dirty black smoke come out the tail pipe," he said. "That thing's an ecological disaster."

"Never mind," she said, stepping up onto the small porch. "It's not forever."

As soon as she had said that word, she wanted to recall it. Gabe's smile faded as he followed her to her door, his expression was bleak and his hands clamped onto her shoulders as he hauled her tightly against him.

"Forever," he repeated. "Forever. Some things, though, you want that way."

She couldn't, wouldn't deny it. "That's right. Some things have to be forever or not at all."

"Kathy, why is it so important to you? Why can't you let this be enough?"

His kiss was rough, tormented, and she took it, gentled it with her own response, made it tender with her own love for him. When his fingers relaxed on her shoulders, curved around them, slid over them, tracked down her back, she laid her head on his chest and held him tightly as they swayed together in an agony of grief that neither could assuage in the other.

"You know it will never be enough," she murmured.

"It could be. It is for lots of people. It was for our parents for damn near twenty years!"

"But not for us." She lifted her head and wrapped her hands around his face. "Gabe, I want to have your babies."

He went still, watchful. "Are you pregnant?" he asked hoarsely.

"No. But give me the word and I'll get that way so fast, your head'll swim."

He took her hands from his face, kissed her palms, and pressed them to his neck where his hot pulse beat against them. "You promised to make this as tough as possible for me, didn't you? And you never were one to hide what you want. You always came right out and said it."

"Do you mind?"

He shook his head from side to side. "No. I think I like the idea of you wanting to have my babies—and telling me so."

"What matters is, do you like the idea of my having them?"

He closed his eyes and pressed his forehead against hers. "I . . . don't think so. When you said that, I don't know what I felt, but mostly it was fear. Because I didn't protect you the other night . . . and I knew it was possible that you were pregnant."

She hated knowing he'd been afraid of her being pregnant with his child. "I'm not," she said shortly, moving away from him. "You don't have to worry about that."

He caught her close, pressing her cheek to his chest. "Dammit, I've hurt you again."

"I should be used to that, shouldn't I?"

"Ah, Kath, don't be bitter toward me. If I could be what you want, I'd do it. I love you. Don't forget that, okay?"

She drew in a tremulous breath and lifted her head. "I won't forget it, Gabriel."

He stood back from her enough so he could see her face in the light from the fixture above the door. "Is there any point in my asking you to come home with me tonight?"

She looked deep into his eyes, but didn't have to say anything at all. His smile hurt her because she knew of the pain it masked. "I didn't think so. Good night, love."

"Good night, Gabe."

He reached around her and opened the door. She hesitated before going inside. "I love you, Gabe. I don't want you to forget, either."

"That's not something I can ever forget," he said, and

walked slowly down the steps. Then, turning, he said, "Done much riding lately?"

She shook her head.

"Want a little practice? I won't be going far or fast. I promised Ricky a day out on his pony, helping me check fences. Will you join us tomorrow?"

Kathy swallowed hard. What was he offering her? A chance to meet his son? Some time with the two of them with a view to seeing what kind of family they'd make together? Or just a day in the saddle, like so many other days they'd spent in years gone by?

Suddenly, she knew it didn't really matter. Whatever it was, it would be better than nothing.

"What time would you like me to be up there?"

He smiled, and something inside her flipped over, taking great gouges out of her heart as it moved. "Seven," he said. "See you." And then he was gone.

Kathy was up and dressed and ready long before seven, but waited until just before that to get into her car and make the short drive over the bridge and up the hill. When she arrived, Gabe was clearly ready for work, dressed in tight, faded jeans, a light jacket, and a sweat-stained Stetson which was pulled low over his forehead. He finished tightening the girth around a big black gelding with a light brown mane and stood erect, watching as she parked beside his truck. Ricky was already astride a small, black and white pony, and a slender strawberry roan stood nearby, cropping the grass around the reins trailing down over her neck. She was saddled and ready for Kathy to ride.

With a small tote bag over her shoulder and a tentative smile on her face, Kathy approached, looking from Gabe to the tiny boy, searching for family resemblance and finding none at all, not a hint of Art's swarthy coloring, or Grace's intensely blue eyes, or the light brown ones Gabe and Rachel both had. Instead, she saw huge gray eyes under thin brows, so fair as to be almost nonexistent, a plump, sun-tanned face, rosy cheeks, and a mop of yellow curls that looked as if they'd deny a brush easy passage. He must, she decided, resemble his mother's side of the family.

"Hi," said Gabe softly, and leaned forward as if he meant to kiss her, but then stood erect, his eyes flicking sideways to the child on the pony. He just grazed her cheek with one bent finger and let out a long breath. "I wasn't sure you'd come."

"I was."

His smile wasn't very secure. "Kathy," he said with great formality, "may I present my son, Ricky." Gabe looked, she realized, scared to death. What did he think she was going to do, take one look at his little boy and run screaming?

"Son, this is Kathy. I told you about her. Can you say hello?"

Ricky gave her a wide grin. "Hi, Kaffy."

Moving forward, she reached out a hand to him. Giving his small brown fist a quick shake, she said, "How do you do? I'm happy to meet you, Ricky. What's your pony's name?"

"Panda. He looks like my bear."

Kathy laughed. "I can see that. I have a bear like that too. Your daddy won it for me at the fair."

Ricky's big eyes opened wider. "What did he do?"

"He hit a milk bottle with a baseball."

"I did not! I popped a whole bunch of balloons with a handful of darts that had tricky weights."

"Yes, you did, and won the red and white dog, but that was a different time."

"Did you go to the fair lots of times?"

"Quite a few, little buddy," Gabe said. Then, shooting a sharp glance at Kathy, he said, "'*Have*' a bear like that?"

"Yes. And the dog. And the pink rabbit. As well as the yellow and white striped snake."

Gabe stared at her. "That thing must have been ten feet long!"

She grinned. "It still is. Lucky for me my dad never wanted to rent out my room when I left home."

"Can we go to the fair, Daddy? Will you win me a big snake?"

"You bet I'll try. I don't do so well without Kathy there. She used to bring me luck." The smile he gave her turned her insides over.

"Kaffy can come too."

Gabe went very still, fiddling with the bridle on the horse he held for her. After a moment, Kathy smiled at Ricky. "Thanks, pal," she said. "We'll see."

As they rode out, Ricky talked incessantly, chatter Kathy enjoyed, amazed at the wealth of knowledge stored in that little head, and at the number of questions he could ask per minute. For much of the time it was left to her to answer those questions because Gabe was busy repairing fence breaks with the roll of wire he carried looped around his saddle horn. To those he couldn't repair on the spot with wire and staples, he tied bright red streamers, leaving them for his crew to repair another day. They checked several hay fields, Gabe explaining that while his cattle ranged free for most of the year, he had to feed them all winter, and so he grew most of that feed.

"Was it difficult, switching from dairy back to beef?"

"Nope. Best thing I could have done. As a dairy farm, the place was marginal. Now it's beginning to show a profit again. What I got selling off the other stock and equipment had to go into setting up again for this."

Kathy looked at his face, half-shadowed by the brim of his hat. "You get some enjoyment out of this, don't you?"

After a moment, he nodded, reluctantly, she thought, as if he hated to admit it even to himself. "There's something kind of like the ocean in the rolling hills, the waving grass. It's . . . okay. I'm contented enough, I suppose."

Around midmorning he galloped his horse up a steep slope back toward where she waited with Ricky. Tilting his hat back on his head, he said, "Who's ready for a break and something cold to drink?" Receiving two smiles in agreement, he led the way to a grassy creek bank where there were tall poplars to shade them, and dismounted, digging a pair of thermoses out of his saddlebags.

"I brought some cookies," Kathy said as Gabe lifted Ricky to the ground.

The boy came closer to her, looking interested. "What kind of cookies?"

"Chocolate chip." She sat down near the bank of the creek.

"From the store?" Ricky was close beside her. "My grammy makes cookies in the oven, but Daddy buys them from the store."

She shook her head in sympathy, handing him the bag. "I baked these this morning, just for you."

"And Daddy?"

She smiled softly, nodding. "Sure. And Daddy."

Ricky took a cookie from the bag and sat down in the grass, very close to her, or possibly just close to the cookies. "Oh, boy! The great big chocolate chips!" He munched. "S'good," he said, spraying crumbs.

Gabe handed him a cup of lemonade, poured one for Kathy, and sat down on her other side, reaching into the bag himself. He took half a cookie at one bite then nodded his agreement. "Very good."

"C'n I have another one, Kaffy?" Ricky was reaching into the bag even as he asked.

Gabe took her hand and held it firmly in his. "You might just have made a friend for life."

She wrapped her fingers tightly around his. "That," she said softly, "is exactly what I'm aiming at."

"You mean to play dirty, don't you, Kath?"

She nodded. "Yup. Real dirty."

He sighed. "What am I going to do about you?"

"Have another cookie?"

"What if you run out of cookies?"

"I'll bake more."

"What if you get tired of baking them?"

"I won't."

"You scare me with this single-mindedness of yours."

"Don't," she said with a sweet smile, "talk with your mouth full. You're setting a bad example."

He flicked out one of the large chocolate chips and held it delicately between thumb and finger, licking it with the tip of his tongue. His glance flicked to the front of her blouse, where her nipples stood out firm and obvious against the cotton. He smiled wickedly. "So," he murmured, "are you."

Kathy spent at least part of each of the next several days with Gabe and Ricky, often having dinner with them, reading Ricky a story at bedtime, or listening to Gabe while he read.

"What are you thinking about so seriously?" he asked, as they walked down the stairs after leaving a sleepy little boy headed for dreamland.

"Pleasure," she said without hesitation. "We both went out searching the world for it. And all along it was here, waiting for us. I'm amazed at how easy it was to find. How simple."

"It isn't, you know." He stepped to the floor and turned back to her, holding her on the bottom stair, their eyes on a level. "Don't be fooled by this. It isn't real, and it won't last." He saw in her eyes that she refused, still, to believe him. It was, he knew, long past the time that he should have told her the truth about himself. If she was so determined to make decisions regarding not only her future but his and Ricky's, now was the time to give her enough information so that she could make a reasoned decision.

"Kathy . . ."

"What?" She kissed him, trying to wipe the serious expression from his face.

"Don't do that."

"Why not? I need to kiss you. I haven't done it since before dinner."

He remembered the kiss they'd shared before dinner, the way it had been curtailed by Ricky's entrance, and submitted to this one, loving the way her tongue slipped so deftly between his lips. "Okay, okay," he said moments later. "Now cut it out. I . . . want to . . . talk to . . ."

"Hmm?"

"I want . . . nothing."

She smiled, tilting her head back, her lips plump and wet and rosy. "You want nothing? You're too easy to please. Go ahead, make it harder for me."

He laughed as he lifted her off the stair, sliding her skirt up so that her legs were free to wrap around his waist. His hands under her bottom moved her slowly against him. She reveled in the heat of them through the thin fabric of her panties. "It doesn't get any harder than this, love."

"Wanna bet?" she whispered as she held on to his neck with one hand and tugged her T-shirt off over her head with the other. She popped the snap at the front of her bra and slipped it down, changing hands so she could free herself of both garments.

Gabe chuckled against her bare flesh. "All right, Madame Houdini, let's see you do the skirt now," he challenged, and she did try, wiggling and shifting against him, her hands finding not the button at her own waist, but the snap at his, not the zipper at her back, but the one at his front.

"Stop that! That's not what you're supposed to be doing," he said with a gasp, but held her up so she could continue doing it. She tickled him and he laughed, his voice vibrating against her ear; he tickled her, and she laughed, her voice purring onto his throat.

"How you doin' with that skirt?" he asked, his words slurred.

"Lift your head out of my way." Miraculously, she had managed to unfasten her skirt. She worked it up her body, over her head, and let it drift to the floor, and Gabe stared at her, wondering if life could get better than this—his woman astride his hips wearing nothing but the tiniest bikini panties and a smile that said she ached for him as much as he ached for her.

"I love you," he said, the pressure building within him until he thought he would burst. She'd been right. It did get harder.

"Yes." Her voice had no substance. Her eyes glowed. Her face and upper body were flushed. He could feel the heat and the moisture of her against his abdomen. "Yes," she said again. "Love me. Now, Gabe," she said in a rush of urgency that he heard and responded to and equaled. And then it was too late to do anything but that which was more necessary than breathing.

On unsteady legs, he made it as far as the living

room where he sat on an armless chair, his hands trembling as he quickly shoved his jeans out of the way, slid her panties aside and pulled her over him, entering her with a thrust that brought glad cries from both of them and tears of gratitude to his eyes. Through them, he watched as her face went taut, her eyes unfocused, her neck rigid, and then he was blinded by the harsh light from within as the spasms inside her massaged him and he slid over the edge to join her.

"Oh, Lord. Oh, Lord. Oh, Lord." From far away, Gabe heard a man muttering those words and knew it was he, but he couldn't stop saying it.

"Kathy. Kathy."

"I know."

"I'm sorry."

Languidly, she lifted her head. "Why?" And let it drop again to his shoulder.

"Oh, hell. Too fast. No time to . . ."

"Savor?"

"Hmm."

"Gabe . . . Savor now."

Somehow, he managed to get them both to the couch where he lay with her in his arms. "I could do this . . ." His voice trailed off.

"Forever?"

He was silent for a long time. "All night."

"Okay, darling. All night."

But when he awoke a little before dawn, Kathy was gone, and so were all her clothes.

"I almost said it," he whispered toward the poplar trees. "I almost said 'forever.' I tried, Kathy. I tried."

It was the insistent, somehow panicked ringing of the phone downstairs that woke Kathy, and she rolled out of bed, rubbing sleep from her eyes, hearing Mike in the shower. Picking up the phone in the den, she mumbled a sleepy hello.

Her greeting was met with a hissing silence, and then there was the sound of a quickly indrawn breath. "Is . . . is Michael there?" asked a female voice shakily.

"Yes, but he's in the shower. May I have him call you?" Kathy was beginning to wake up.

There was the sound of a sob, quickly choked off, then the woman spoke again, "Look," she said, breathing quickly, "I don't know who you are or what you're doing in Michael's house at this time of day, but you have to get him out of there! He's in danger!"

"What? Wait, let me get him, just hold—"

"No! No! There's no time! I have to leave again right this minute, but tell him, tell him, please, to get out of there. Out of his house. Out of town. To go away. He's in danger, I tell you!"

"Please! Who is this? What's your name?"

"Just tell him! There's no time to waste!" The woman was sobbing in earnest now, her voice broken and choked, words nearly impossible to decipher. "Tell him to go, to leave his house, to get to safety!"

"But why? What's wrong? I'll tell him, of course, but please, give me more information, or he might not do it! Your name!" What was this, some kind of crank call? They were the bane of a country newspaper editor's life, she knew, but there was something about this hysterical woman's voice that made her wonder if perhaps this call was genuine. There was something too urgent about her words, and cranks didn't usually cry.

"Oh, please, please, if you care for him at all, you'll do as I ask. Oh, Lord. He'll be killed! I beg of you, get him out, make him leave. If you can influence him at all, get him to saf—I can't take any more time.

Just go!" The frantic voice was cut off abruptly by the click of the phone as it was hung up, and Kathy stood there staring at the instrument in her hand.

She heard the shower shut off and went to the bathroom door. "Dad, I think you'd better get out here fast. There's something very wrong."

"I'll call Rachel," he said, as soon as Kathy had finished her tale. "Are you sure it was Grace?" Mike was leafing through a small black indexed book.

"No. Not absolutely. It's nearly fourteen years since I've heard her voice. But she was crying. Who else would be so upset about someone hurting you?" She shivered. "Daddy, maybe you better get out of the house. What if there's a—"

"Kath, make coffee."

"Yes," she said, but she stood right beside him, unable to move, except for the trembling that had taken hold of her limbs.

"Hey, don't take this so seriously." Mike gave her a stern shake. "It probably was just a crank call. You know they come by the dozen every year." As he spoke, he punched out numbers on the phone. "You'll see. And even if it wasn't, nobody's going to get close to your old dad. Now, go make coff—Rachel. It's Mike. Is your mother all right?"

Kathy heard her old friend's voice thin through the phone. "What do you mean, is she all right? Of course she is. Why wouldn't she be?" Rachel's coldness chilled her. Of course that was why there'd not even been a secondhand hello.

"Because I think I just got a phone call from her, and she didn't sound all right to my daughter."

"Kathy? Kathy's there? Why? Because of Gabe?"

"Dammit, Rachel, there's no time for social chatting. Just go and get your mother. I need to be certain she's all right."

"She's asleep. It's six o'clock in the morning, for

pete's sake! And she doesn't want to talk to you. Can't you understand that? Can't you leave her alone? Haven't you hurt her—all of us—enough?"

"Rachel, get her!" Something about Mike's urgency must have gotten through, because she murmured assent, and there was a tense silence as Kathy and Mike stared at each other, waiting, Kathy clinging to her father.

"Mike?" It was a wail of terror. "She's gone! Mike, my mother's not here and her car's not out front and there's a note on her bed. Art has escaped, and she thinks he's headed back to the valley!"

Ten

"Dad . . . Gabe. We have to call Gabe!" Kathy's eyes were wild. "And then we have to get out of here. Grace is right. If Art's headed this way, he's after you."

"Kath—I don't run. But you're right. Gabriel has to know about this. You go get dressed. I'll call him. Go. Now!" he insisted when she hesitated.

Kathy went, knowing he was right. Whatever was going to happen, she'd face it better in something other than a cotton housecoat.

"Damn!" she heard Mike mutter as she ran back down the stairs. "Where the hell can he be? Doesn't he have a phone in that damned barn?"

She dashed to the window at the sound of a vehicle pulling in and nearly sagged with relief. It was Gabe. His hair was wild, as if he had just gotten out of bed, and his chin was bristled with whiskers. Under his arm, he carried Ricky, who seemed to think it was funny that Daddy was running and carrying him. Flinging open the door, Kathy said, "Gabe, your mother just called and—"

"I know. I heard from Rachel. Listen, I want you

and Mike to come up to the farm with me now. The police are on their way here, but it would be better if you were out of the house. Get anything you might need, and let's move out. Now." He set Ricky on his feet but kept a hand on his shoulder.

"No," said Mike calmly, scooping coffee into the basket of his percolator. "Grace is coming here. I don't go anywhere until she arrives. But you're right, Gabe. You and Kathy and Ricky shouldn't be here. The fewer people available in a possible hostage-taking situation, or whatever Art plans, the better."

"Dad! Are you out of your mind? You can't stay."

"I stay until Grace gets here. I don't want her facing that lunatic alone."

Kathy sat down. "If you stay, I stay."

"Now listen," he began, but was interrupted by a quiet, calm voice from the doorway.

"Everyone stays."

The silence was profound. Ever after, Kathy would remember it as a timeless, motionless moment. Gabe stood nearest the door, with his face tortured as he looked at his brother. Ricky was at his side, his eyes big and confused, looking from one adult to another as if seeking reassurance. Mike stood at the counter, the coffee scoop poised between canister and pot. And she sat on a chair with her bare feet curled up underneath her, feeling the breeze from the open window at her back, hearing normal sounds of vehicles on the street, birds trilling, someone calling a child for breakfast. Art, oddly pale, stood behind her father with the doorknob in one hand and a short, black gun in the other.

Slowly, the tableau shifted. Art shut the door with unhurried calm, his hand left the doorknob, and his arm reached out. He clamped a fist around Ricky's arm and snatched him—making the child squeal with fright—to a position in front of his legs.

"Daddy!"

"Daddy," said Art sarcastically. "I'm your daddy, boy."

Mike set the percolator onto the back burner of the stove, turned on the heat, and said, "Let the boy go, Art. I'm the one you came for, right?"

"No. Not only you. It's her too. We'll wait. You said she's coming. That traitorous bitch Andrea called her, I suppose. I thought she'd called you." Art's gaze flicked sideways to Gabe.

"Somebody called me before Rachel did," he said. "I didn't get to the phone in time. Who was it? Andrea?"

"Andrea. Bitch. She'll die, too, but not until I'm finished with her. Like your mother."

"You won't touch her," Gabe said quietly. "You'd never hurt Mom."

"She's not my mother! She's a whore!"

"She raised you. She loves you. She never stopped caring for you no matter what you did."

Art spared his brother another brief glance. "She betrayed me. She betrayed my father's memory. How can you forgive that?" He fixed his dark eyes on Mike's face. "With you. She went with you."

"Not while your father lived. Never then."

"She wanted to. You were younger. My father was old. She wanted a young man. And when he died, she went with you. She betrayed his memory. They're all the same. Women." He looked at Kathy, and she froze at the madness in his eyes. Madness and malevolence—and he had Ricky.

"But he betrayed me. It was mine. My farm. She got to him, made him do it, and he left it to her— her and her brats."

"And you," said Mike. "The farm was more yours than anybody's."

"Right! And you made sure I couldn't have it,

didn't you? You got me out of the way. So you could have her, and he"—he tossed his head sideways toward Gabe—"could have my land!"

"I didn't murder those people for you, Art. You did that yourself."

"I had to! Don't you see?" Art's voice became plaintive. "I had to. She was just the same. It was her fault. I saw her around town. She was in the hardware store, and she looked at me." His face grew sly. "You know the way a woman can look at a man, so he knows."

Mike nodded. Kathy saw a look pass between him and Gabe. She interpreted it as, *You keep him talking, and I'll jump him,* and wanted to cry out to Gabe not to try it. He'd said the police were on their way. They might even be out there, right now, waiting for a break in order to make a move. With her eyes, she pleaded with him, but he studiously avoided her gaze, keeping his pinned on his brother.

"She wanted me," Art continued. "I saw her again a day or two later, and she looked at me like that again, so I followed her. I knew what she wanted."

His fist tightened around the gun, his eyes squeezed shut for an instant as if he were in pain, and Gabe started to move, freezing when Art opened his eyes, fixing them on him as if he knew.

"Then what happened?" asked Mike quickly, taking Art's attention back to himself.

"Then she pretended she didn't want it. They do that, you know. Women."

"And so you killed her." There no censure in Mike's tone, just quiet understanding.

"I had to! You have to understand that. She was bad. She shouldn't do that to a man. And she wouldn't stop screaming." His tone was bewildered. "Why are women like that? Why do they do those things to us?"

"Grace isn't like that, Art. Grace doesn't do things like that."

"Grace . . . No." His smile was filled with love, like a little boy thinking of his mother. "She doesn't do things like that. Where is she? She's here, isn't she? Mom? Where are you? You're hiding her. Why are you hiding her? I loved her best. And she loved me until she had those babies, then she didn't love me enough anymore. I want to see her. I miss her so much." His face crumpled, and he began to cry, his hand loosing its grip on Ricky, coming up to wipe his face, but his other hand still held the gun, and his glittering, tear-filled eyes never wavered from Mike.

Kathy saw Gabe poised to move again, saw him hesitate because Ricky still stood there in front of Art, though no longer pinned by that big hand, and terror gripped her. From her position on the far side of the table, she couldn't reach the child, but she beckoned to him, and he, seeming to sense the necessity of silence, crept away from Art, ducked under the table, and came to her.

With shaking hands, she clasped him, lifted him as she stood and thrust him out the open window, letting him drop even as she dropped back into her chair, looking as innocent and as inconspicuous as she could so that when Art's crafty gaze swung to her, there was nothing for him to see.

Ricky's howl of outrage was quickly stilled, and a female voice said, "Hush! Don't cry. Come to Grammy."

"Kaffy frowed me out the window!" he complained.

"Yes. Kathy's very smart. Let's go."

Suddenly, Art sniffed, wiped his eyes dry, and, with the gun still squarely on Mike, never wavering, he took a quick glance at Kathy's side of the room. "Where is the boy?" he demanded.

"What boy?" said Gabe. "There is no boy."

"Andrea said—" He shook his head, confused. He looked at Gabe. "Andrea's just the same, you know. She's a slut. She was mine, and she married someone . . ." He rubbed the back of his free hand over his forehead and gnawed on his lip. "You! She married you! And there was a boy! He's mine and you took him!"

The instant he swung the gun away from Mike, Gabe acted. He lunged across the kitchen and grabbed his brother's hand. He shoved it high. Art grunted and forced it down, down, down, while Gabe struggled silently against the force of Art's muscle and desperation. Again, for Kathy, time stood still as Gabe and Art wrestled in slow motion. Up the gun went, and then down, out to one side, then it was hidden between them, and then up in the air again.

There were grunts and curses and the sound of feet scuffing on the floor, and then a flat, not very loud sound as the two men went crashing down.

Someone screamed.

There was blood on the floor, pooling, pooling, redder than she'd imagined blood could ever be. Shiny. Wet. Growing.

Men came pouring through the doorway, each one leaping to one side as he did so, standing crouched, guns pointed, braced on wrists, and a voice barked, "Freeze right there!" Someone screamed "Mike!" and there was scuffling on the porch as Grace broke free of restraint, leapt into the room, and flung herself into Mike's arms.

Slowly, Gabe got to his feet, looked down at the body on the floor, and turned his back. He folded his arms on the wall, laid his head against them, and said, "I killed my brother. Oh, God help me. I killed him!"

The explanations came out over a period of hours,

as they were interviewed separately and then as a group by the RCMP.

Andrea would have to face charges for her part in assisting Art to escape, but the punishment she received could well be tempered by the fact that she had tried to warn the family when she realized where Art wanted her to take him. And why.

Grace, unable to sleep, had been sitting close beside Rachel's phone when the call came. Rather than waste time with the argument she knew she'd get from her daughter and son-in-law, and the danger Graham would have to face if he accompanied her, she simply left, knowing it would be useless to phone Mike before morning.

No one knew better than she how soundly he slept, she added with a smile. He sat now with his arm around her, and she clutched his hand tightly in both her own.

"I'll sleep a lot more soundly now that you're home, my girl," he said, and Grace turned a lovely shade of pink.

"Girl?" she asked.

"Girl," he said flatly. "My girl."

"What happened then, Mrs. Fowler?" Gently, the officer called Grace's attention back to her.

"After I called and talked to Kathy . . ." Grace smiled again, "though I didn't know it was her, I got back in my car and drove. Where were you people?" she demanded of the policewoman. "I drove like a maniac, and there wasn't a soul around to give me a ticket." Or help me, was the unspoken accusation.

"Mrs. Fowler, why didn't you phone the police as soon as you heard from your daughter-in-law . . . er . . . Andrea?"

"What? Oh! It didn't occur to me. How strange. I just wanted to get here, to Michael, and not waste time. And I wanted to stop Art from doing anything more to anyone else." She drew in a shuddering breath and bent her head over hers and Mike's clasped hands, her tears falling softly. "And at that, I was much too late. Oh, my poor boy. He wasn't really bad, you know. Just . . . sick. Why couldn't I have saved him too?"

There was a funeral, of course. It was quiet, attended only by family. There was an investigation, but no blame was laid in the death of Arthur Fowler, escaped mental patient. His fingerprints were the only ones on the gun, and his death was termed an accident.

Throughout both ordeals, Gabe, pale and quiet, said little to anyone.

"He's grieving," Grace told Kathy. "You just have to let him go through it in his own way, in his own time."

"I know, but he's shutting me out."

"He's shutting me out too," Grace said sadly. "He did the same after his father died. All you can do is wait, and be there for him if he needs you. When he needs you."

But Gabe, it seemed, didn't need her. He went through the motions, did necessary chores around the ranch, rode out with his men to mend fences, check stock, cut hay when it ripened, and baled it for winter feed. He didn't neglect his son, but Ricky wanted to spend more time with Kathy and his grammy and Mike than with his daddy.

"Daddy doesn't have fun anymore," he said sadly, then cheering up, added, "But I have fun with you."

Kathy hugged him tightly.

Grace was a lucky bride. The sun shone on her as she and Mike were joined in matrimony in the yard by the house where she had raised her family.

Rachel stood at her side, and roses filled the air with perfume. Gabe, at Mike's side, was solemn throughout the ceremony but cheerful enough during the luncheon reception. And when the bride and groom left in a shower of rice, Kathy rejoiced to hear him laughing with Ricky and little Danny, as they watched the chickens he had let out scramble to get their share of the feast. When the guests were gone, Rachel and Kathy, friends again, changed into comfortable clothes and, with Graham and Gabe, cleaned up. Then, as the two old friends hugged each other tearfully, Graham loaded both his babies into the car, put his nephew in between them, and patiently waited for his wife to join him.

"Good-bye, good-bye," Rachel called, leaning out the window and waving. "Come and see us soon! Come with Gabe when he comes down for Ricky next weekend."

Then, suddenly, they drove out of the yard, leaving Kathy and Gabe alone. It was something she had been longing for—and dreading—and now that the time had arrived, she didn't know what to say. Neither, it seemed, did Gabe.

"Well," he said. "All over."

"Yes. All over. It was a good wedding, Gabe."

"I suppose so." He drew in a deep breath, let it out gustily, and then smiled at her, the taut, strained smile she'd become used to in the past weeks.

"Kath . . . will you come for a ride with me?"

She didn't hesitate, but linked her fingers with his. "Sure. Where do you want to go?"

"Just away from here."

They rode the horses slowly over the fields. They had been ambling along for nearly an hour before Kathy realized where he was taking her.

The little lake glimmered blue and silver through the branches of a tree—the maple where their initials were carved. The grass grew long and lush and thick there, and it was dotted with constellations of white daisies and comets of pink fireweed. As they dismounted and walked toward the water's edge, a killdeer shrieked and flew up in front of them, then hobbled away with a mock-broken wing. Sharing a smile, they played the little bird's game, and followed her, away from her nest in the grass.

Sitting down, backs against the big tree trunk, they were silent for a long time. Then, reaching out, Gabe took Kathy's hand and wrapped it in his own.

"Thank you," he said.

"For what?"

"For giving me this time I needed. I know you must have thought I'd stopped loving you."

"I never thought that, Gabe. I know you were hurting. I wish there had been some way I could have helped."

"Is there any way anyone can help a man who killed his own brother?" he asked.

"It was an accident, love."

"Was it? Most of the time, I'm sure of it, but I wonder in the dark of the night, if it was."

"You were trying to take the gun from him so he couldn't kill again. It went off. It could just as easily have been pointed at you when it did."

She shivered and moved closer to him, glad he was alive, aware that had things gone differently, they might not be sitting there now. It was a terrible thought.

"He wasn't even after me, so I can't claim self-defense."

"It happened, Gabe. And never forget that he would have been after you. If he had killed Mike, then you and I, like the husband of that poor woman, would have had to die too. He was beyond reason. In a way, he was no more responsible than you were. It was, like the investigation showed, an accident. But he caused it; you didn't."

"But that's just it, Kathy. I did cause it. Just as I caused the death of that young couple four years ago."

Kathy pulled away from him and knelt before him, shocked, staring into his eyes. "That's insane! You weren't even here! How could you be guilty of that?"

He brought her back to his side and laid a heavy arm over her shoulders. "I told you all my dreams once, Kathy. And I told you all my nightmares. What I didn't tell you was the truth. The truth is, Art killed long before he killed those two campers. He murdered our father, and I suspected it and didn't say anything to a soul."

"Oh, my darling, no!" She wrapped him in her embrace. "You were eleven years old! Gabe, you must have been mistaken. A tractor rolled on him. Art couldn't have done that!"

"Art did do that. He tampered with the tractor and one of the wheels fell off as Dad went around the side of a steep slope, just as Art had hoped. I found him there after Dad had been taken away. He was repairing the tractor so that no one would ever know."

"He told you that?"

"No. Of course not. But even at eleven, I knew enough to realize Art wouldn't be messing around with that tractor at that moment unless he had something to hide."

"Did you ask him what he was doing?"

"No." A spasm of pain crossed his face. "I knew what he was doing, and I was too afraid to even let him know I'd seen him. I was sure, if I did, he'd kill me, too, and maybe Mom and Rachel. I was always so afraid of Art."

"Because he bullied you constantly. But Gabe, that didn't make him a murderer."

"No. But you know he was one."

"Not your father's murderer."

"He was."

"But why? For heaven's sake, Gabriel, why? He loved your father! You always said that. You always said that no matter how rotten Art was to anyone else, he loved your mom and dad, and you had to remember that."

"It was what I told myself. In order not to hate myself completely. Only . . . it never really worked. That was what drove me away from here as much as Art's treatment of me did. And why I said I'd never want to settle down with anyone."

"With me," she said.

He nodded. "With you." His jaw clenched. His scar puckered. He forced himself to meet her eyes. "You've always had so damned much integrity, Kath. You don't lie, and you don't play social games. Hell, if you so much as get some extra change in a store, you give it back. I've known that about you forever. And since you came back, it's been worse. You told me right out you loved me. You said you wanted me. You said you wanted to have my babies. You hid nothing, and I've been hiding so much. So, how can I ask you to share the life of a guy who was too much of a coward to tell the truth about his own father's murderer?"

"Or a guy who never told the truth because he was sure he wouldn't be believed, and even if he was believed, would have caused a lot of hurt to his mother and sister who were already going through the trauma of having lost a husband and father. Think of that, Gabe. Think of what you spared them. Think of that eleven-year-old kid carrying that burden all alone. Have some pity for him, show him some kindness in your thoughts. Love him a little. Because I love him a lot.

"And while you're doing that, give some consideration to the thought that maybe, after all, that little boy was wrong. What motive did Art have to kill your dad?"

"I didn't know it then, but since I've been back, I've been in a position to go over the books for all the years past, and I think I've finally found that elusive motive. You see, beef prices had dropped drastically that year, and he wanted to go into dairy, but Dad refused. That's all there in Dad's journals. Art was sure dairy was the answer, and that Dad's methods of using the land would lead to the loss of the ranch. All he cared about was the land, the property, and he was willing to do anything to preserve it. Even kill his own father."

"Whew! Yes. All right." Kathy believed him, suddenly. Believed that the interpretation he had put on Art's actions with the tractor had been the right one. It wasn't so farfetched to anyone who had known Art, but still . . .

"Gabe, you can't blame yourself for that or for anything else that he did."

"I'm an accessory."

"You were a kid!"

"If I had told, maybe he'd have been stopped."

"And maybe no one would have believed you."

He touched her face tenderly. "You do. And you were afraid of him too." He hugged her tightly. "The look on your face when he grabbed Ricky. It was as if he had touched your own child."

"In a way, he had. He was touching the child of your heart."

"Yes. And, as the woman of my heart, you'd feel that." For the first time in weeks, a genuine smile lit his face, though with a hint of tension still hiding behind it. "You really don't despise me, do you?"

She shook her head.

"You never would have, would you? If you'd known."

"No."

"If the investigation had showed that I killed him, knowing what you do about what he did to my dad and how I feel about the death penalty, would you still be here with me?"

"Yes, Gabriel. I promise you. I'd be with you. But it's over now, and now you can start to forget."

"Yes." He smiled into her eyes, love shining out of his face, doubts dwindling until they were gone. "With your help, I'll forget."

She leaned into him. "You got it, sailor. All the way."

"Right here?" he murmured several moments later, his heart pounding hard in his chest, his body aching with need. "Right now?"

"Right now. Right here. There is so much magic in this world, love. Share it with me."

"This magic is only between you and me," he said, and then slowly began the long climb to where it lived within both of them. When it was over, and they lay side by side in the thick grass, she wished for the courage to tell him that the sun was shining, not the stars, and that the magic had never been stronger.

"Will you stay with me tonight?" he asked when they had finished a late dinner of leftovers from the wedding feast.

Kathy walked into his arms. "I'll stay with you tonight and any night you want me to," she whispered. "For just as long as we have."

With a groan, Gabe carried her up the stairs to his bedroom, and they loved long into the night.

When Kathy awoke, she was alone, and the cool sheets beside her told her Gabe had been up for a long time. A shaft of sunlight lay across the floor, and she stepped into it, reaching for his shirt to wrap around herself. It smelled of his body, and she hugged it close to her skin. The carpet was warm underfoot, and she stood there for several moments, looking out the window at the quiet, pastoral scene, expecting to see Gabe riding by on one of his morning duties.

When he didn't appear, she wandered down the stairs, into the bathroom, and then out into the kitchen. There wasn't even a pot of coffee made, she noticed, and proceeded to make one. Where could Gabe have gone?

She had finished one cup of coffee and had started on a second, when he appeared at the door. "Oh, good, you're up," he said. "Come outside. I have something to show you." Like an eager boy, he dragged her to her feet.

"Hey, wait! All I'm wearing is this shirt, you know. I can't go outside with a bare—"

"Bottom?" he asked. "If I remember correctly, you had more than a bare bottom exposed yesterday down at the lake."

She laughed and let him drag her toward the door. "That was different. You have men working here."

"Not today. There's no one here but us."

He towed her onto the porch, down the steps, and into the yard. "Now look up," he said, and she tilted her head back.

Up there was a dome of blue sky, a few puffy clouds that didn't mean anybody any harm, and a hundred thousand stars of all shapes and sizes, cut from aluminum foil. Stars hanging from strings running between the house and the barn. Stars dangling down from wires strung from the shed to the house and to each tree. Stars flipping back and forth in the breeze. Stars hanging from the eaves and from every branch and limb and twig. And each one caught the light of the sun, twinkling crazily in the daylight, then blurring behind the tears that filled Kathy's eyes as she laughed and cried and reached for the man she loved.

"Oh, Gabe! This must have taken you hours!"

"Hours well spent," he said, wiping her face with the palms of his hands. "Don't cry, my darling. Be happy with me. Be happy with me for the rest of our lives. Marry me, Kath. Marry me soon, and we'll look at starry skies both day and night."

"Yes," she said, lifting her face to his. "Oh, yes."

Hours later, as the firelight glinted on the string of hanging stars they had brought inside with them, Gabe lay propped on one elbow on the quilt they had spread on the living room floor, staring at her as she lay on her side.

"What are you looking at?" she asked.

"The stars," he said. "The ones in your eyes."

"You're entitled. You put them there."

"I mean to see they stay there too. Forever, Kath."

Slowly, she nodded, and whispered, "Forever, Stargazer. Just for you."

THE EDITOR'S CORNER

As is the case with many of you, LOVESWEPT books have been a part of my life for a very long time—since before we ever published book #1, in fact. Having worked with Carolyn Nichols for over seven years, there's no way I could not have been caught up in her enthusiasm for and devotion to the LOVESWEPT project. I hope I can convey my excitement over the wonderful books we publish as entertainingly as Carolyn has over the years in the Editor's Corner.

Since next month is April, we're going to shower you with "keepers." Our six books for the month are sure to coax the sun from behind the clouds and brighten your rainy days.

Continuing her *Once Upon a Time* series, Kay Hooper brings you **WHAT DREAMS MAY COME**, LOVESWEPT #390. Can you imagine what Kelly Russell goes through when, a week before her wedding, her fiancé, John Mitchell, has a tragic accident which leaves him in a coma? Ten years later Kelly is finally putting the past behind her when Mitch arrives on her doorstep, determined to rekindle the love that fate had stolen from them. Kay involves the reader from page one in this poignant, modern-day Rip Van Winkle story. Your emotions will run the gamut as you root for brave survivor Kelly and enigmatic Mitch to bridge the chasm of time and build a new life together.

Sandra Chastain has the remarkable ability to create vivid characters with winning personalities. Her people always lead interesting, purposeful lives—and the hero and heroine in **ADAM'S OUTLAW**, LOVESWEPT #391, are no exceptions. Toni Gresham leads a group of concerned citizens called Peachtree Vigilantes, who are out to corral muggers who prey on the elderly. Instead she swoops down from a tree with a Tarzan yell and lands atop police captain Adam Ware! Adam, who is conducting his own sting operation, is stunned to discover he's being held captive by an angel with golden curls. You'll laugh as the darling renegade tries to teach the lone-wolf lawman a thing or two about helping people—and in return learns a thing or two about love.

I suggest saving Janet Evanovich's **SMITTEN**, LOVESWEPT #392, for one of those rainy days this month. There's no way that after reading this gem of a romance you won't be smiling and floating on air! Single mom Lizabeth Kane wasn't exactly construction worker material, but she

(continued)

figured she could learn. The hours were good—she'd be home by the time her kids were out of school—and the location—the end of her block—was convenient. Matt Hallahan takes one look at her résumé—handwritten on spiral notebook paper—then at the lady herself, and he's instantly smitten. When the virile hunk agrees to hire her, Lizabeth's heart—and her libido—send up a cheer! Lizabeth never knew that painting a wall could be a sensual experience or that the smell of sawdust could be so enticing, but whenever Matt was near, he made her senses sizzle. Janet adds some zany secondary characters to this tender story who are guaranteed to make you laugh. For an uplifting experience, don't miss **SMITTEN!**

April showers occasionally leave behind rainbows. Tami Hoag brings you one rainbow this month and two more over the next several months in the form of her three-book series, *The Rainbow Chasers*. The Fearsome Foursome was what they called themselves, four college friends who bonded together and shared dreams of pursuing their hearts' desires in a sleepy coastal town in northern California. In **HEART OF GOLD**, LOVESWEPT #393, Tami picks up on the lives of the friends as one by one they realize their dreams and find the ends of their personal rainbows. Faith Kincaid is just about to open her inn and begin to forget her former life in Washington, D.C., when elegantly handsome Shane Callan—Dirty Harry in disguise—arrives on assignment to protect her—a government witness in a bribery trial. Faith has never known the intoxicating feeling of having a man want her until Shane pulls her to him on a darkened staircase and makes her yearn for the taste of his lips. Shane, lonely and haunted by demons, realizes Faith is his shot at sanctuary, his anchor in the storm. **HEART OF GOLD** is a richly textured story that you won't be able to put down. But Tami's next in the series won't be far behind! Look for **KEEPING COMPANY** in June and **REILLY'S RETURN** in August. You can spend the entire summer chasing rainbows!

Courtney Henke is one of the brightest new stars on the LOVESWEPT horizon. And for those of you who wrote after reading her first book, **CHAMELEON**, asking for Adam's story, Courtney has granted your wish—and delivered one sensational story in **JINX**, LOVESWEPT #394. How much
(continued)

more romantic can you get than a hero who falls in love with the heroine even before he meets her? It's Diana Machlen's ethereal image in an advertisement for the perfume her family developed that haunts Adam's dreams. But the lady in the flesh is just as tempting, when Adam—on a mission to retrieve from her the only written copy of the perfume formula—encounters the lovely Diana at her cabin in the Missouri Ozarks. Diana greets Adam less than enthusiastically. You see, strange things happen when she gets close to a man—and there's no way she can stay away from Adam! The chain of events is just too funny for words as Adam vows to prove her wrong about her jinx. Don't miss this delightful romp!

Deborah Smith's name has been popping up in more and more of your letters as one of the favorite LOVESWEPT authors. It's no wonder! Deborah has an imagination and creative ability that knows no bounds. In **LEGENDS,** LOVE-SWEPT #395, Deborah wisks you from a penthouse in Manhattan to a tiny village in Scotland. At a lavish party billionaire Douglas Kincaid can't help but follow the mysterious woman in emerald silk onto his terrace. Elgiva MacRoth wants the brutally handsome dealmaker—but only to kidnap him! She holds him captive in order to preserve her heritage and convince him to give up his land holdings in Scotland. But soon it's not clear who is the prisoner and who is the jailer as Douglas melts her resistance and revels in her sensuality. These two characters are so alive, they almost walk right off the pages. Deborah will have you believing in legends before you finish this mesmerizing story.

Look for our sparkling violet covers next month, and enjoy a month of great reading with LOVESWEPT!

Sincerely,

Susann Brailey

Susann Brailey
Editor
LOVESWEPT
Bantam Books
666 Fifth Avenue
New York, NY 10103

FAN OF THE MONTH

Kay Bendall

What a thrill and an honor to be selected a LOVE-SWEPT Fan of the Month! Reading is one of the joys of my life. Through books I enter worlds of enchantment, wonder, adventure, suspense, beauty, fantasy, humor, and, above all else, a place where love conquers all.

My favorite books are LOVESWEPTs. Each and every month I am impressed and delighted with the variety and excellence of the selections. I laugh, cry, am inspired, touched, and enjoy them all.

Kay Hooper, Joan Elliott Pickart, Iris Johansen, Deborah Smith, Barbara Boswell, and Peggy Webb are some of my favorite LOVESWEPT authors. The blend of familiar and new authors ensure that LOVESWEPTs will remain innovative and number one among the romance books.

The day the mailman brings my LOVESWEPTs is my favorite day of the month!

OFFICIAL RULES TO
LOVESWEPT'S
DREAM MAKER GIVEAWAY
(See entry card in center of this book)

1. NO PURCHASE NECESSARY. To enter both the sweepstakes and accept the risk-free trial offer, follow the directions published on the insert card in this book. Return your entry on the reply card provided. If you do not wish to take advantage of the risk-free trial offer, but wish to enter the sweepstakes, return the entry card only with the "FREE ENTRY" sticker attached, or send your name and address on a 3x5 card to : Loveswept Sweepstakes, Bantam Books, PO Box 985, Hicksville. NY 11802-9827.

2. To be eligible for the prizes offered, your entry must be received by September 17, 1990. We are not responsible for late, lost or misdirected mail. Winners will be selected on or about October 16, 1990 in a random drawing under the supervision of Marden Kane, Inc., an independent judging organization, and except for those prizes which will be awarded to the first 50 entrants, prizes will be awarded after that date. By entering this sweepstakes, each entrant accepts and agrees to be bound by these rules and the decision of the judges which shall be final and binding. This sweepstakes will be presented in conjunction with various book offers sponsored by Bantam Books under the following titles: Agatha Christie "Mystery Showcase", Louis L'Amour "Great American Getaway", Loveswept "Dreams Can Come True" and Loveswept "Dream Makers". Although the prize options and graphics of this Bantam Books sweepstakes will vary in each of these book offers, the value of each prize level will be approximately the same and prize winners will have the options of selecting any prize offered within the prize level won.

3. Prizes in the Loveswept "Dream Maker" sweepstakes: Grand Prize (1) 14 Day trip to either Hawaii, Europe or the Caribbean. Trip includes round trip air transportation from any major airport in the US and hotel accomodations (approximate retail value $6,000); Bonus Prize (1) $1,000 cash in addition to the trip; Second Prize (1) 27" Color TV (approximate retail value $900).

4. This sweepstakes is open to residents of the US, and Canada (excluding the province of Quebec), who are 18 years of age or older. Employees of Bantam Books, Bantam Doubleday Dell Publishing Group Inc., their affiliates and subsidiaries, Marden Kane Inc. and all other agencies and persons connected with conducting this sweepstakes and their immediate family members are not eligible to enter this sweepstakes. This offer is subject to all applicable laws and regulations and is void in the province of Quebec and wherever prohibited or restricted by law. In order to win a prize, residents of Canada will be required to correctly answer a time-limited arithmetical skill-testing question.

5. Winners will be notified by mail and will be required to execute an affidavit of eligibility and release which must be returned within 14 days of notification or an alternate winner will be selected. Prizes are not transferable. Trip prize must be taken within one year of notification and is subject to airline departure schedules and ticket and accommodation availability. Winner must have a valid passport. No substitution will be made for any prize except as offered. If a prize should be unavailable at sweepstakes end, sponsor reserves the right to substitute a prize of equal or greater value. Winners agree that the sponsor, its affiliates, and their agencies and employees shall not be liable for injury, loss or damage of any kind resulting from an entrant's participation in this offer or from the acceptance or use of the prizes awarded. Odds of winning are dependant upon the number of entries received. Taxes, if any, are the sole responsibility of the winners. Winner's entry and acceptance of any prize offered constitutes permission to use the winner's name, photograph or other likeness for purposes of advertising and promotion on behalf of Bantam Books and Bantam Doubleday Dell Publishing Group Inc. without additional compensation to the winner.

6. For a list of winners (available after 10/16/90), send a self addressed stamped envelope to Bantam Books Winners List, PO Box 704, Sayreville, NJ 08871.

7. The free gifts are available only to entrants who also agree to sample the Loveswept subscription program on the terms described. The sweepstakes prizes offered by affixing the "Free Entry" sticker to the Entry Form are available to all entrants, whether or not an entrant chooses to affix the "Free Books" sticker to the Entry Form.

THE DELANEY DYNASTY

Men and women whose loves an passions are so glorious it takes many great romance novels by three bestselling authors to tell their tempestuous stories.

THE SHAMROCK TRINITY

☐	21975	RAFE, THE MAVERICK *by Kay Hooper*	$2.95
☐	21976	YORK, THE RENEGADE *by Iris Johansen*	$2.95
☐	21977	BURKE, THE KINGPIN *by Fayrene Preston*	$2.95

THE DELANEYS OF KILLAROO

☐	21872	ADELAIDE, THE ENCHANTRESS *by Kay Hooper*	$2.75
☐	21873	MATILDA, THE ADVENTURESS *by Iris Johansen*	$2.75
☐	21874	SYDNEY, THE TEMPTRESS *by Fayrene Preston*	$2.75

THE DELANEYS: *The Untamed Years*

☐	21899	GOLDEN FLAMES *by Kay Hooper*	$3.50
☐	21898	WILD SILVER *by Iris Johansen*	$3.50
☐	21897	COPPER FIRE *by Fayrene Preston*	$3.50

Buy them at your local bookstore or use this page to order.